CHANGE
OF
HEART

CHANGE
OF
HEART

•

Sandra D. Bricker

AVALON BOOKS
NEW YORK

© Copyright 2001 by Sandra D. Bricker
Library of Congress Catalog Card Number: 00-193457
ISBN 0-8034-9475-0
Published by Thomas Bouregy & Co., Inc.
160 Madison Avenue, New York, NY 10016

PRINTED IN THE UNITED STATES OF AMERICA
ON ACID-FREE PAPER
BY HADDON CRAFTSMEN, BLOOMSBURG, PENNSYLVANIA

For Mom.
You're a true believer.

And to Debby and Page
with love and thanks
for every one of the 37,318 times
one of you said, "Oh yes, YOU CAN!"

And to my T.A.R.A. girls (and boy),
and all my writer-buds, online and off.
It doesn't get any better than you!

Also, very special thanks to Erin,
for all the free therapy and writer-sitting.
You're a very patient person.

Chapter One

Sage stepped out of taupe sandals with four-inch heels. Dangling them from two fingers, she eased open the front door and slipped quietly inside. The grandfather clock stood tall and imposing in the foyer, and she cringed at its message. 5:45 A.M. She'd made a habit of staying out late most of her adult life, but this was outrageous, even for her!

Her only hope was that her father had retired early and would never know she'd been out all night. Even at twenty-eight years old, her father's "my house, my rules" attitude had inspired Sage in her own brand of rebellion: keeping her pursuits of entertainment as separate from her home life as possible. Coming back as an adult to live beneath her father's roof, and what felt like his scrutiny of every aspect of her life, had been a difficult adjustment to make. But it wasn't as if she had a choice, really. Where else was she going to go?

1

Setting her sandals on the third stair, she padded cautiously across the oak-stained floor toward the kitchen, the spandex of her short and glittering, copper tank dress making a soft whooshing sound as she moved. The low growl from her stomach urged her on, and she pushed the ornately carved door at the end of the hall open in search of satiation.

She stood in the frame of the open refrigerator and peered inside, wiggling the toes of her sore bare feet, and tending to her stiff back with a long, catlike stretch. Wrapping wild, flame-red curls that hung halfway down her back into submission around her hand, she fashioned a makeshift bun and tied it into a knot as she considered her options. Leftover roast beef . . . a bowl of cold broccoli . . . a half-eaten cheesecake.

Removing the roast platter with one hand and grabbing a carton of orange juice with the other, she pivoted toward the counter.

"You must be Sage."

The words stunned her, breaking the silence of a day not yet begun, and Sage dropped the carton of orange juice, helplessly watching it clatter to the floor and spill across the Spanish ceramic tile. The platter of beef toppled at the edge of the counter, and she pushed it backward to safety with her hip before reeling around to find the source of the voice.

"I didn't mean to startle you," the man continued.

"Wh-who are you?" Sage asked finally, her eyes wide and questioning.

"Ben," he replied, as he approached her and extended his hand. "Ben Travis."

Sage took his hand half-heartedly, her emerald green eyes narrowing curiously. "Do I know you?"

"I'm here with Elizabeth," he continued. "From the orphanage?"

"Ohhhh," she replied, and then grimaced. "I'd forgotten you were going to arrive today. Daddy must be livid with me for missing your welcome dinner."

"I don't think so." Ben squatted to mop up the juice with a wad of paper towels. "He didn't seem to be, anyway."

Sage leaned back on the counter and watched him for a moment. His light, sandy hair was mussed, giving him a casual edge that matched the gray sweatpants and black T-shirt he wore over what appeared to be very well-developed muscles in his chest and arms.

"We have people who will do that," she offered. "Just leave it for Cook."

"Nonsense," he said as he shook his head, and Sage was momentarily captivated by his glistening blue eyes. "I can do it."

"Well . . ." she began, but she didn't know where to go from there. "I was going to make a sandwich," she told him finally, pointing at the platter of roast beef. "Would you like one?"

"No." He sighed, tossing the wad of juice-soaked towels into the trash can beneath the counter. "It's a little early for me. I just came in search of coffee."

"Oh."

Sage felt suddenly nervous as she faced his inquisitive gaze. "Well . . . there's the coffeepot," she pointed out. "But you're on your own. I don't have a clue how to use it."

"You don't make coffee?" he asked, and she noticed the slight twitch at the corner of his very appealing mouth.

"I don't drink it, and I don't make it," she informed him. Was that judgment she sensed swimming around in the blue of Ben Travis's eyes? "You're sure you don't want a sandwich?"

"I'm sure," he told her, then moved easily about the kitchen preparing a pot of coffee while she tended to her sandwich.

Sage wrapped the masterpiece in sourdough with a paper towel and headed for the doorway, leaving the platter of meat and all of the fixings out on the counter.

"Well," she told him over her shoulder as she left, "make yourself at home. If I don't see you before you leave, it was nice to make your acquaintance."

"You, too," Ben replied, after she'd already moved out of earshot. Shaking his head at the mess she'd left behind, he picked up the platter and the condiments and moved them back to their place in the refrigerator as the aroma of fresh coffee began to waft through the kitchen.

Sage yawned as Dodie, a servant in her family's home since Sage was a child, set down a steaming china cup before her.

"Your tea, Miss," Dodie said quietly, removing the brunch plate from before her. "Shall I serve your usual?"

"No," Sage told her with a shake of her head. "I'm not very hungry this morning. Just a scone with cream."

As Dodie moved away, Sage's gaze met Ben's, and they both seemed to linger for a frozen moment.

"Don't you agree, Sage?"

Sage forced her attention back to her father, who was expectantly waiting for a reply.

"I'm sorry," she said, smiling her best smile in her father's direction. "What did you say, Daddy?"

"Sage, I'm afraid you're being very rude to our guests."

She sighed apologetically. "I am sorry," she directed at Beth. "I'm so sleepy this morning."

"Nonsense, Mac," Beth grinned, rubbing her hand over the top of his. "Sage hasn't been rude in the least. I do hope to spend a few minutes in your mother's garden, though, dear. And I hope you will indulge me by coming along."

Sage wanted to groan, but her love for Beth, combined with her desire to get back into her father's good graces, ruled out over her desire for sleep.

Beth always had a cause to spur her on. If Sage wasn't so desperate for her four-poster bed and big old feather pillow, she might have been able to regard the woman with a bit of envy. Everything she did in her life seemed to really *matter*, and no cause she championed was too small for the full focus of her loyal efforts.

"Of course," she nodded. "Why don't we go now?"

"Will you gentlemen excuse us?" Beth asked, and Mac and Ben both rose from their chairs.

"It's fine work you're doing in Mexico," Sage heard her father say as they exited. "Beth tells me you're very committed."

Commitment. Oh, how her father must love to see that in a stranger visiting his home! He'd lamented the lack of it in his own daughter often enough, after all.

"How your mother loved these gardens," Beth sighed, slipping her arm inside Sage's as they walked the path.

Roses of every shade and type bloomed in each direction, and just the sight and scent of them pinched unexpectedly at Sage's heart. She hadn't been to the garden in months, but now that she was there, her mother's presence whispered to her as warmly as it ever had before.

"She had a gift, really," Beth continued. "She could always make things grow."

Sage didn't say anything as she stared at the tea roses against the white picket fence.

"I'm sorry I haven't been around much this last year," Beth told her. "I know it must be a very difficult time for you."

Sage shrugged slightly, then patted the top of Beth's hand and smiled. "I'm all right."

She really was all right too. Yes, she'd unexpectedly lost her mother to a cancer she never knew she had . . . and yes, she'd made a sudden break from the altar on the day of her intended marriage to Stephen Cooper . . . but she was all right. She would survive. And here, in the shelter of her childhood home at the marina in San Diego, she had healed and carved out a new life for herself. She had friends, she had her father, she had a roof over her head, and she basked in the security of knowing that she would be taken care of for as long as she needed to be. Her world was safe. Uncluttered. Simple.

And then there was Eric.

Eric's portfolio was a Wall Street dream. His import/export business was a thriving artistic conglomerate, and his taste in clothes, art, gourmet cuisine, and social culture was impeccable. Sage loved the way he doted on her, and she could see a future with Eric that involved very little compromise. They were well-suited to one another: He, the caregiver and provider, and she the gentler influence to his hectic life.

Once she finally brought him around to her way of thinking and Eric proposed, Sage knew that their combined assets would create a formidable presence in San Diego's most elite circles. At one time she'd hoped for that with Stephen. Until she had panicked. And then bolted, hiking up her wedding dress and letting her veil fly into the wind behind her as she fled. Then there had been no turning back. Stephen would have nothing to do with her after that. But Eric would do nicely in his place, she realized now. She could still have everything she'd hoped for.

". . . And the work they're doing down there would just warm your soul, Sage."

She flinched to realize she hadn't heard a word Beth had said since they sat down together on the old wrought-iron bench.

"You always have something to be passionate about," she told Beth honestly. "Always someone new to help. Some cause to champion. Mother loved that about you."

"What else are we here for?" Beth smiled, and Sage could see such vibrance behind the older woman's graying eyes.

She remembered Beth when she was young—her mother's dearest friend on earth—and Sage realized she didn't look very different now. Just less of her raven-black hair apparent beneath the silver tresses, and a few more lines upon her rose-petal skin. Even the pure blue of her once-crystalline eyes was still visible at times.

"This orphanage is home to more than twenty children, Sage," Beth continued. "Children with no families. No parents. And until they came to Ben, no hope."

"So Ben is some sort of savior to the children," Sage said, sighing. "Why would he devote his life to this work? Is he independently wealthy?"

"Goodness, no." Beth chuckled. "Ben is a missionary of sorts. He raises money from the private sector in order to keep things going down there."

"A missionary!" Sage exclaimed. "He's far too cute to be a man of God!"

"Why, Sage," Beth gently chastised. "Men of God can be handsome. Strong. Creative."

"None of them that I've ever seen," Sage interrupted with a chuckle. "Until Ben Travis."

"As long as you're sensing an attraction to him, you might do well to get to know Ben better while we're here," Beth suggested. "He's been single for three years, since his wife died down in Mexico. He's a man of dignity and fine moral value, Sage."

"Not to mention poverty," Sage added with a shake of her head. "No, I think I'll stick with Eric. He and I are meant to be."

"It's not that I didn't enjoy meeting Eric when I was here in January, honey," Beth said, as she affectionately smoothed the curls at Sage's temple, "but is he capable of being a spiritual leader to you, to your future children?"

"I appreciate your concern," Sage said softly, and then took Beth's hand into hers. "You're such a dear. But that sort of thing just isn't as important to me as it is to you. Eric will be a good provider, and he treats me like a queen. Those are the things that matter most to me."

"You had such great faith as a child," Beth replied and Sage sensed a tinge of regret in the woman's eyes. "And you were such a big dreamer!"

"I remember." The memory was a sweet one for Sage.

"What happened?"

Sage paused thoughtfully for a moment, then slid her arm into Beth's and lowered her head to the woman's shoulder.

"Life happened," she whispered, the glint of tears momentarily obstructing her vision. "Just life."

Chapter Two

Saying good-bye to Beth was harder than Sage had anticipated. She was surprised to battle an onslaught of tears as she stood arm-in-arm with her father and watched Beth and Ben disappear down the length of the driveway.

"How about a sunset cruise around the bay?" Mac suggested as they wandered back toward the house.

"That would be lovely," she replied, "but I'm meeting Eric at the gallery and we're going out tonight."

"Out again tonight," he commented. "Burning the candle at both ends makes for a very weak candle, my dear."

"Oh, Daddy," she sighed. "I'm young and I'm in love. Surely you can remember what that's like."

"Let's see," Mac teased. "Can I remember back that far? There were dinosaurs and I carried a big club. Yes, ah yes, and I was in love! Yes, I can remember back to those ancient times."

"All right," she grinned. "There's just no talking to you sometimes." And with a peck to his cheek, Sage set off toward her black Miata parked outside the garage.

"I'll see you before sunrise?" he added as she turned over the ignition, and Sage could sense the serious edge beneath the question.

"Yes, Daddy." She beamed, and he predictably softened. She knew just how to talk to him when he became like this; it worked every time.

Sage cranked up the radio and sang along with Aerosmith as she sped along The Strand toward downtown. With the convertible top down and the air full with salty Pacific moisture, Sage felt the sense of freedom she had been craving ever since Beth had arrived with Ben Travis. She didn't know what it was about their visit, or even whether Ben had anything to do with it at all, but she had experienced a restlessness with them at the house. She'd felt like an animal backed into a corner, and once they had driven away she'd sadly and quietly escaped.

She took the corner at full speed and squealed to a stop in the alley outside Antiquities. The dark-haired Latino man that Eric had parking cars for the gallery arrived at her door in an instant. Sage took a moment to smooth the wrinkles from her silver satin pajama pants and adjust the black, short-cropped crocheted sweater topping them before swinging open the enormous glass doors.

"Good evening, Miss McColl," said the trendy girl with the big eyes who greeted gallery patrons.

"Good evening," Sage replied. She was ashamed to realize she didn't know the girl's name, despite the fact that she'd been working for Eric the whole six months they'd been dating. "Is Mr. Randolph in the back?"

She didn't wait for a reply before breezing into the back office and closing the door behind her.

"What am I interrupting?" She grinned as she greeted Eric with a quick kiss on the lips.

"Final inventory of today's shipment of goods," Eric's assistant Graham answered for him. "You two go on ahead. I can finish up from here."

"Well, if you're certain," Eric said, then dropped his pen and paperwork to the tabletop at Graham's nod of confirmation. "We have reservations at La Traviata," he told Sage as he led her toward the door. "Would you like to stop by Firestorm for some dancing afterward?"

"It sounds heavenly," she told him when they stepped outside. "But I'm on thin ice with my father right now. I need to make it an early night."

The Latino man opened the passenger door of the silver Lexus, and Sage slid inside.

"You're an adult woman, Sage," Eric impatiently observed. "Isn't it about time you set your own curfew?"

Sage waited for him to slip behind the wheel, then ran a hand over his arm as they drove away. "It just makes my life easier to play the game by his rules when he gets like this," she assured him.

"All right," he conceded. "Just dinner then."

The couple was seated at their usual table, set inside an exquisite bay window overlooking the harbor, and Sage settled into the plush leather chair.

"What do you feel like tonight?" Eric asked her, without looking up from the menu. "I'm thinking mussels."

"Mussels sound good."

Eric was the picture of authority and power to Sage, and she watched him intently as he ordered for them both. His six-two, two hundred-pound frame completely filled the massive chair across from her, and his dark eyes and hair crowned his impeccable appearance. No one wore Halston like Eric Randolph.

"So how was business today?" she asked curiously.

"Same as every other. Have the holy rollers taken leave of your home yet?"

"Yes," she said, snickering. "They left this evening just before I came to meet you."

"Honestly, I don't know why Mac indulges Beth, with her insistent pleas for the depletion of his fortune. One underprivileged sob story after another. The woman was born giving to the poor."

"He indulges her," she said, trying not to sound offended, "because she was my mother's childhood friend. She's like part of the family. And Beth has a huge heart. She sees a need, and she wants to do something to fill it."

"A regular Mother Teresa," he said snidely. "With her hands moving deeper down into Mac's pockets with every visit."

"I wouldn't worry about Daddy if I were you," she assured him as the appetizers were set out across the table. "His pockets are deep enough to endure it."

Sage had the feeling that Eric was going to respond but thought better of it. She was just as glad. She wasn't in the mood to hear anything bad about Beth just then. Her departures were always fairly regrettable, but, for some reason Sage could not quite discern, this one had seemed particularly disturbing. It had been freeing, yes, but then a foreboding loneliness had set in while she wasn't looking.

Ben Travis crossed her mind out of nowhere just then, but she dismissed him and returned her focus to Eric.

"I have to go to New York on Saturday," he said. "Perhaps we can . . ."

The incessant beep of his pager stopped him mid-sentence, and Sage tapped her foot as she waited for him to check it before resuming.

". . . make a little trip of it," he continued, producing a cell phone from the breast pocket of his charcoal suit coat.

"That would be wonderful," she nodded excitedly. "I haven't been to the city in ages. There's this little bistro I found there when I . . ."

"What is it?" He cut her off when someone picked up his call.

Sage was used to being cut off by cell phone conversations and annoying pages, by business associates and over-accommodating waiters. Eric's time was in high demand, and she inwardly acknowledged her great fortune at being in a position to attract so much of it for herself.

"I have to run back to the gallery," he said, as he flipped off the phone and returned it to his pocket. Then, catching the eye of the waiter, he added, "Can we make this a quick one?"

The waiter nodded and rushed off to the kitchen, which seemed to somewhat appease Eric, and his face relaxed.

"What is it?" Sage asked him. "Is something wrong?"

"When is there not something wrong on the day of a

new shipment?" He shrugged in resignation. "I don't know why I pay Graham the kind of money I pay him when he can't seem to do anything for himself."

Dinner was finished in less than thirty minutes, and Eric was on his feet the moment he'd signed the credit card receipt. "I'm sorry, muffin. I've got to get a move on."

By the time Sage had risen, Eric was already at the door of the restaurant. Noticing that he'd left his pager on the tabletop, she snatched it up and dropped it into the pocket of her trousers, then hurried to join him curbside. What did he do when she wasn't there to pick up after him?

Eric chattered quietly on his cell phone all the way over to the gallery. Sage felt just a bit abandoned when he pecked her on the cheek and abruptly left her by her car in the alley to rush off and take care of whatever disaster it was this time that demanded his full and immediate attention.

"Duty calls once again," she said, sighing, and slid into the Miata to dig in her purse for the keys.

It wasn't until she clicked the seat belt buckle into place and her hand brushed the block of plastic in her pocket that Sage remembered Eric's pager. He would absolutely explode if she knowingly left without returning it to him.

Not that he would even have it if it weren't for me dutifully retrieving it from the restaurant table, she reasoned, as she climbed back out of the car and headed into the gallery. *For such an important businessman, he certainly is disorganized.*

Once inside, Sage headed straight past the maze of

exhibits toward the well-lit office in the back. She could hear that Eric seemed agitated, and she thought she wouldn't want to be where Graham was standing at just that moment.

"How could you make such a mistake?" Eric seethed as she approached the doorway. "Manchester is expecting me to produce the Vesper Diamond on Thursday. You idiot!"

The Vesper Diamond.

The words stopped Sage cold. A cacophony of news program highlights slid across her brain. The Vesper was a gargantuan black diamond: over one hundred carats in its polished state, if she remembered correctly. It had been stolen from an Indonesian art exhibit several years prior, and occasional spottings from time to time had provided fodder for mystery buffs and magazine news shows.

Eric had the Vesper Diamond? The notion reeled about inside her mind until Sage could barely contain the thoughts.

"How are we going to explain this? This is a criminal element we smuggle for, Graham. They aren't going to take kindly to our misplacing part of their product."

"It isn't misplaced. It's just in one of the other crates."

Graham's quick nod drew Eric's attention to where Sage stood, frozen and stunned.

"What are you doing there?" Eric shouted. "Are you spying on me, Sage?"

"N-n-no," she stammered. "I-I . . . Y-y-you f-forgot your p-pager . . ." She produced it from her pocket, then clumsily dropped it to the floor.

Eric gently placed his clipboard on the desk and

looked at her powerfully. "Now I suppose that was a most unfortunate case of eavesdropping."

"I w-wasn't," she insisted. "I just happened to . . ."

She fell instantly silent as Eric headed for her, retrieving his pager from the floor in front of her.

"Oh, this is just *great!*" Graham exclaimed, slamming his fist on the desk. Sage's gaze turned for the first time to the fire burning in Eric's dark eyes.

"My God, Eric. What have you done?"

She was sorry the moment the words left her lips.

"See there," Graham said. "You can't trust her to keep this quiet, Eric. Look at her face. If you let her leave here, she's gonna spill this to anyone who happens by her on the way home!"

Eric scowled at her for a moment, and Sage felt the blood inside her veins run instantly cold.

"N-n-no," she assured him, backing away. "I won't."

Eric snatched her by the arm before she had the opportunity to consider what to do, and dragged her into the office so roughly that the sleeve of her crocheted sweater began to unravel.

"You are a bit of a chatterbox, aren't you?" he growled at her as his eyes darted about the room in a search she didn't understand.

"You want me to take care of her?" Graham offered, and Sage whimpered slightly at the thought.

"Open the closet door," he ordered, then he shoved her inside and slammed it shut.

"Eric, please!" she shouted from the dark enclosure as she pounded on the door with both fists. "Let me out of here right now!"

18 *Sandra D. Bricker*

"Quiet!" he bellowed from the other side of the door. "Let me think."

"I can take care of her," she heard Graham offer again. Sage wanted to punch him one time really hard as repayment for his eagerness.

"Eric, *pleeeease!*"

After a lengthy pause, she heard Eric tell Graham to get rid of her car, and the fading sound of clanking keys. Sage's mind raced with a mixture of revelation and sheer terror. When the closet door finally opened, she realized that her face was wet with anxious tears.

"Wrong place at the wrong time, muffin." Eric shrugged, and she thought for the first time that he looked quite dastardly. Why hadn't she noticed that about him before?

"I'm caught between a rock and a hard place," he continued, as he moved toward the desk.

Sage surveyed her surroundings as quickly as she could between his glances. The door was closed, probably locked. The windows were barred. No chance at getting to the phone.

"I can't trust you not to tell anyone what you've seen and heard here tonight," he went on. "And yet . . ."

Her instincts kicked in at that one, slow-motion instant. She realized that Eric kept a gun in that desk drawer. And now he was heading for it. She had to do something, or she could be dead in a moment's time.

". . . I had so hoped to continue amusing myself with you for a time . . ."

She waited until the moment he lowered his gaze—just before his hand rested on the handle of the desk drawer.

"Eric, no," she cried, flying toward him and snatching up the heavy Mayan vase on the pedestal to his left.

"*Nooooo!*" she screamed, then hit him hard over the head with the vase so that it smashed into a gazillion splintered pieces. Eric crumpled to the floor.

Sage watched him for a moment, hopeful that he wouldn't move. He didn't, so she rushed to the office door, flung it open, and ran out through the gallery. When she slammed against the barrier of the glass doors, locked from the outside, she screamed in frustration. Without a second thought, she picked up the Egyptian sculpture she had always loved so much, and tossed it straight through the front window.

The gallery's alarm shrieked as she climbed through the broken glass and hurried haphazardly over the shattered remains of Eric's prized sculpture, once worth nearly half a million dollars.

Serves him right, she thought as she ran down the street. *Lock* me *in a closet, will you!*

Chapter Three

The events of the twenty-four hours which followed her ordeal ran through Sage's mind like a movie trailer shown in full Technicolor. She'd conveyed her story so many times, first to her father, then to the police, then to her girlfriend Connie who came to the house as soon as she'd heard.

By the time the ambulance had arrived to take Eric to the hospital for medical care, he was nowhere to be found. Only a thick pool of his blood was left behind, and three lone diamonds no more than a single carat each. Just enough evidence to corroborate her story, both to the authorities and within her own mind. She'd asked herself a hundred times whether she'd been dreaming.

There had been no sign of Graham since then either, and the detective in charge of the case revealed to Sage and Mac that Eric Randolph had been under suspicion of smuggling rare stolen artifacts for at least six months.

The diamonds were a new revelation. There had been departmental leaks, false information, and bumbled operations to slow the progress along the way, but none of them were surprised to hear what Sage had to say. In fact, they were relieved. They now had three tiny sparkling pieces of evidence as well as one shaken witness.

"Ms. McColl, please reason with your father," one of the detectives had pleaded, unconsciously running his hand through thick black waves of perfect, early-Elvis hair. "We will protect you, see that nothing bad happens to you from here on in. But you're the only one who can bring Randolph out of hiding. If you work with us, it will be fast and painless."

"For whom!" Mac wouldn't hear of such an idea. Using his daughter for bait? Over his dead body, he had vowed. And now Sage stared out the window of the car as it thumped down a remote and dusty red clay road.

"If we're going to do this," he had said, "I'm going to be in charge of Sage's safety. I know a place where Randolph would never think to look for her."

"Please," the detective had repeated. "If she stays in sight, with our protection twenty-four hours a day, we can draw him out. How long are you willing for your daughter to remain in hiding, Mr. McColl? How long?"

"As long as it takes for you to do your job and capture Eric Randolph," Mac had replied authoritatively. "My daughter is not the criminal. She is the victim."

And so here she was. In a dilapidated junk-heap with a stranger she felt certain didn't speak a word of English, on her way into the remotest hills of Mexico. Only God knew what she would face upon arrival. Would there be room for her? Were there bathtubs or showers, or indoor plumbing at all for that matter? She tried to recall Beth's tales of the orphanage in sharper detail, but she couldn't manage it. She made a mental note to work on her listening skills in the future.

Tears stung Sage's eyes at the uncertainty of her fate, and she turned her gaze away from the man driving her straight into it, whatever it would turn out to be. Would everyone at the orphanage know why she was there, that she was hiding out from her criminal boyfriend who had tried to kill her?

What will Ben Travis think of me now?

She didn't know why it mattered so much at that moment, but it did. She dreaded facing him under these circumstances.

Sage pulled down the sun visor, but there was no mirror attached. She rummaged through her purse until she found her compact, then used the mirror to tuck in the free-flying wisps that had escaped from her ponytail. She noticed that her eyes were nearly as red as her hair, and dark circles corroborated her intense feelings of exhaustion. If only she had her four-poster bed and lovely feather pillow. She was sure she could sleep for a week.

The driver muttered something to her in Spanish, and Sage shrugged.

"I don't speak Español," she told him, and he nodded seriously before returning his focus to the road.

Sage's imagination began to run wild as her heart started to race inside her.

This man could easily drive me out into the middle of nowhere. He could rob me, beat me, or worse! How do I know I can trust him? Oh, what has my father sent me into?

And just about the time she thought she might give in to the panic, the driver took a sudden turn and skidded down a dusty embankment to the road beneath. On the other side of the bone-dry trees, Sage could see the crude rooftops of several one-story buildings.

"Is this it?" she asked, and the driver nodded in reply.

At least a dozen children of all ages surrounded the car as it came to a stop at the center of their little village home. They were a sea of dirty faces and tattered clothes, hopeful smiles and dark, shining hair. When Sage unfolded herself from her filthy chariot, a few of the children took her by the hand and began leading her to the nearest of the buildings.

She peered over her shoulder to see the driver unloading her two bags, abandoning them in the road before peeling out of the village without so much as a look back in the rearview mirror. When he had disappeared from sight, Sage brought herself back to the situation before her. Just as she reached the entrance to the building, Beth appeared in the doorway and shot her a smile. Sage began crying almost immediately.

"Oh, my dear Sage!" Beth exclaimed emotionally, wrapping her up in a wholehearted embrace. "Are you all right? Let me look at you. Did he hurt you?"

"No," Sage managed to say, still clinging to Beth, and irritated with herself for trembling so violently. "I'm not hurt."

"Your father had no time to give the whole story," Beth said, as she thumbed the curls at Sage's temples, a familiar and soothing act she had been performing as long as Sage could remember. It never failed to bring her comfort. "But right now you look exhausted. Let me show you to our barracks."

"Barracks?" Sage asked as she went along obediently. *Have I joined the Army?*

Sage was surprised when she awoke to find the sun settling down for the day. She had to have been asleep for three hours or more; even on a folding cot with a scratchy wool blanket, she'd given in to her fatigue.

She sat up on the bed and looked around at her surroundings. Cinder blocks and concrete shaped the walls, and the dirt floor had been surprisingly camouflaged with a layer of patted-down straw and a torn area rug at the center. Each of the beds was sharply made up, and she assumed that the steel cabinets hid her personal items, of which she could find no trace.

Sage's attention was drawn to a slight rustle in the corner. She smiled at the frightened child looking back at her through enormous brown eyes.

"Hi," she said softly. Then, "I mean, *hola.*"

The little girl stared back at her in silence, no acknowledgment of her in the least.

"Como está usted?" Sage struggled. High school Spanish class was little more than a distant memory. *"Como se llama?"*

"Coco," the child replied.

"Hi, Coco. I'm Sage," she told her, and the little girl turned and ran as fast as she could out of the building.

"Great," Sage sighed as she rose from the cot. "I'm scaring the orphans."

Sage wandered out of the barracks and a welcome balmy breeze caressed her face. She stopped for a moment to take in a deep breath, and she thought she felt the twinge of the salt air of home in her nostrils. Oh, how she missed San Diego just then.

"We've got fish tacos for supper tonight. If you want to eat, you'd better get over there soon."

Sage's heart began to race, pounding enthusiastically against the inside of her chest before she had even turned to confirm that Ben Travis was standing nearby.

"Do you ever make any noise when you enter a room?" she asked him. "It seems you're always startling me."

"From now on, I'll wear a bell."

They exchanged brittle smiles, and Sage was compelled to look away.

"Thank you for taking me in," she said, just above a whisper.

"It's the least I could do," he told her. Then he added, "But you'll earn your keep here, I assure you."

Sage raised an arched brow at him and he grinned brightly.

"There is a lot to do here, Sage. And as long as you're here, you'll be working right alongside the rest of us."

"Fine," she offered half-heartedly. "It's only fair."

But she didn't mean it completely. After all, she'd just been through the ordeal of her life, and she needed a safe place to rest and recover.

I should have known he'd jump at the chance to harbor me in this horrible place. Daddy's probably paying him well. And, of course, he gets a free slave out of the bargain! If he thinks for one minute that I . . .

"Come on," he said, then walked away from her toward the building glimmering with yellow light. "Hope you like fish tacos."

"I've never heard of them," she replied, but he didn't stop or look back. She almost had to run to catch up to him. Once they were inside the cafeteria he left her side and Sage found herself standing alone.

"You're up!" Beth exclaimed as she hurried toward her. "I saved you some dinner. Take a seat at the head table, and I'll fetch you a plate."

Sage tried to return the uneasy smiles of dozens of children who watched her like a firefly in a glass jar. The little girl she'd met earlier, Coco, followed her at a safe distance all the way up to the front of the room. Once she was seated, the children seemed to lose interest in her a bit, returning to their giggly conversations and contagious laughter.

There's nothing like the laughter of a child. It's like some sort of song.

One such child drew Sage's attention, and she noticed that Ben was seated on the bench beside the boy. They were conversing easily in Spanish, and they burst into full guffaws simultaneously before Ben gave the boy a rumpled pat on the top of the head and moved to the next table for a while.

He had an admirable nonchalance with the children that drew Sage's unconscious scrutiny, and she could see that he was well-loved and deeply respected in this child-sized world to which he'd chosen to devote himself. There was a certain purity in that devotion. Sage thought she could better understand that now, as she watched him interact with the wards of his commitment.

"Here we go!" Beth sang as she set a plate before Sage.

Fish, tartar sauce, and lettuce wrapped in thick corn tortillas. There were two of them on Sage's plate alongside a runny scoop of black beans.

"It's Mexican fast food," Beth said as she sat down beside Sage. "Like Fish McTacos!"

Sage grinned, and then shrugged slightly. "Here goes nothin'," she offered before taking a bite. "Hey, it's not so bad," she admitted as Ben stepped up to the table. "It's actually pretty good."

Ben graced her with a brief smile, then nodded toward Beth. "Can I have a minute?"

Beth rose, squeezing Sage's shoulder as she eagerly followed Ben toward the kitchen.

Sage took a few more bites of the meal, then noticed Coco standing nearby watching every move she made.

"Hi," she offered, then patted the chair beside her in an invitation for the child to join her. As she had done before, Coco flushed, then hurried away as quickly as her little legs would carry her.

"Something I said?" she asked Beth when she returned to the table.

"She's just shy," Beth explained. "And the children find you . . . fascinating."

"Fascinating? Why?"

"Your red hair," she revealed. "These children haven't seen many blonds or redheads."

"Oh." Sage nodded. "I hadn't thought of that. So what was the big secret with Ben?"

"Well," Beth began, then paused self-consciously. "He wanted to make sure you were aware . . . I mean, not today, mind you, because this is your first day, after all . . . but in the future . . ."

"Spit it out, Beth! For goodness' sake."

"Well, Ben is concerned that you've led a rather sheltered life, Sage. He's worried that you won't be able to fit in here at the orphanage."

"Did he say that?"

"Well," Beth grimaced. "He saw me serve you your meal . . ."

"And he reprimanded you?"

"No," she assured her, then took a deep breath. "He doesn't know you like I do, honey. He only knows the home he's seen in San Diego, with the manicured garden and maids to cook and serve. He just wants to make sure you know you won't be served while you're here. I told him that you're well aware . . . that you can learn to do things for yourself . . ."

That self-absorbed, judgmental creep! Does he have any idea what I've been through?

"And tonight we'll go over your list of chores for your stay here," Beth added reluctantly. "It won't be so bad, honey. You'll see. You'll feel like it's home in no time at all."

Feel at home with Ben Travis anywhere near, within a thousand miles? she asked herself angrily. *Never!*

Chapter Four

Sage had been peeling potatoes for what seemed like a week. Her fingernails were chipped, her knuckles were bleeding, and she knew she must look a fright! Her stubborn hair was coaxed back into a reluctant ponytail, and the long strands that had escaped were hanging down around her face.

There had been no time for makeup that morning when she was torn from her sleep at the crack of dawn, and she'd thrown on the first thing she could find through blurry eyes and a still-sleeping brain. But now it was hot, and she was exhausted from working in the kitchen all morning long. Blue jeans had been a poor choice, and she made a mental note to find a mall at some point and purchase several more pairs of shorts for this odyssey.

Sage resented the surge of response to Ben's entrance, and, although she forced her attention back down to the million potatoes in the sink before her, she didn't stay that way for long. Ben looked like a commercial for golf clubs, or a top-of-the-line four-wheel drive vehicle, in khaki shorts and a striking hunter green knit shirt. As always, he was surrounded by chattering children. The man moved through the camp like the Pied Piper, for heaven's sake!

"That was a quick trip!" Beth greeted him. "Everything go well?"

Sage looked on with interest, despite the fact that she hadn't known he'd left camp that morning.

"We're still negotiating," he said as he shook his head. "We may have to be a bit creative in finding our own answer." His smile of acknowledgment toward Sage brought about an odd self-consciousness in her that set her heart to pounding and her hands to fidgeting. "Afternoon." He nodded her way.

"H-hi."

"That's a shame," Beth continued. "I was so hoping they would be moved to make it easier on us. If not for the gringos, at least for the children. Their children."

Sage was so keenly aware of her reaction to this man that every nerve ending in her body seemed to dance inside, taunting her. What was it about him that made her entire being fade to mush?

Steeling herself against another one of those smiles, she returned her attention to the potatoes. She wasn't quite sure she'd ever master the task, but she was going to give it one hundred percent of her focus, that was for sure. At her next scrape of the peeler, a chunk of potato flew over the edge of the sink and onto the floor at Ben's feet.

"Ouch!" she squealed, blood oozing where she had

also peeled away a good bit of skin from her index finger.

Ben hurried to her and looked at the wound. Without a word, he took her by the hand, led her to a bucket of clean water on the wooden table behind her, and dipped a cup inside.

"Quit squirming," he said, then poured the water over her finger to cleanse it. "Beth, do we have the first-aid kit?"

"Yes, I'll fetch it."

"It's fine, really," Sage insisted gently.

"Have you ever peeled a potato in your life?"

She couldn't discern whether his question leaned more toward judgment or sheer amusement.

"Yes," she snapped.

"Yes?" he asked. "You've peeled potatoes." His words took the form of an incredulous accusation.

"Yes!" she repeated.

"When?"

Sage's blood boiled. Okay, she was lying. But did he have to hound her this way?

"A long time ago."

"A long time ago," he repeated. "Well, from the looks of things, I'd say a *very* long time ago."

"Here we go!" Beth breezed in before Sage could respond. She didn't know what she would have said anyway.

She watched Ben intently as he doctored the wound with antiseptic cream. Her heart lurched a little at the way he rested her hand over his to treat it, and then it lurched a lot when their eyes met for a heated, endless moment.

"Beth will wrap it," he said, breaking the silence between them. And before she could respond, Ben let her hand drop from his and was on his way out of the kitchen.

"She'll need a bandage," he commented to no one in particular, without even looking back. "And she might think about cutting those fingernails. There are no fashion shows in this neck of the woods."

"Cut my fingernails indeed!" She seethed as Beth wound gauze around the joint of her finger. "He is infuriating! I just want to go home!!"

"Ben's not so bad." Beth grinned. "And you know you can't go home until your father gives the all-clear sign. It's too dangerous for you."

"Oh, I know," she groaned. "But he is impossible."

"You two just have to adjust to one another. He doesn't know you like I know you yet."

"I don't suppose he ever will," Sage replied, grimacing.

"Oh, he will. And to know you is to love you, my dear."

Beth's sweet smile comforted Sage, and she breathed a heavy sigh, resolving to put Ben Travis completely out of her mind, once and for all.

Ben's usual pace had increased from a comfortable jog to an all-out run as he headed into the sunrise up the long stretch of beach he had come to know so well. Mornings had become his favorite time since he'd come to Mexico. His morning run, and then an hour or so of devotions on the rocks above the sand, had become a ritual.

Today he reached his spot in record time, and he fell to the boulder, breathless, his heart pounding and his teeth grinding. Everything about Sage McColl set him on edge.

The muscles in his jaw were twitching out of control as he opened his Bible and began to read the same passage three times over. Finally, he closed the book with a groan.

He released a long, shaky sigh.

"What is it about her?" he whispered toward the watercolor sky.

Shaking his head, Ben brought himself back on track. He rubbed the aching skin of his forehead, then stopped to watch the glittering gold reflection of the sea.

After a few more moments of quiet time on the edge of the ocean, Ben was renewed. He pushed his Bible down into his small leather backpack, slipped it over his shoulders, and continued his run down the border of the beach. A thousand pounds were lifted off him, he realized. Or perhaps just about one hundred and forty.

Yes, Sage probably weighed about that.

Sage had never wanted children. Those pangs people spoke of in movies and romance novels were completely foreign to her. The idea of expanding beyond normal human capacity, only to have an eight-pound turkey force its way out of your body, was more torture than she ever wanted to bear in this life. And then to raise the little bird, from diapers and throwing up, to toddling and more throwing up, and finally on to puberty, where, no matter how outstanding a parent you might actually be, your turkey would undoubtedly rebel against you in every conceivable way. Why on earth would people go to such outrageous lengths to bring something so overwhelming into their lives? It never made much sense to her.

Oh, sure, kids were fine. They repopulated the planet, and they were something to coo over when getting together with girlfriends she hadn't seen in a long time. Better to focus on what they'd produced than on what had happened to their bodies along the way anyway. Children could even be quite adorable at rare moments throughout their formative years, Sage acknowledged, as she watched several little girls chasing each other through camp. But to change one's life to revolve solely around a child's personal needs and desires while your own dreams fell victim to voluntary deprivation? Why?

When they'd told Sage, at age twenty-one, that she would probably never conceive, she'd simply nodded, accepting her fate. Despite the fact that her mother reacted as if the end of the world had been declared, Sage herself hadn't been devastated, nor was she inspired to spend a gazillion dollars on alternative possibilities. It wasn't going to affect her in any dramatic ways, since she had never wanted to become one of those sacrificial mommies that seemed to litter the highways of life, pushing their children to live out the dreams they themselves had grown so far from along the way. It just wasn't the stuff your average movie-of-the-week was made of, but she made no apologies.

Now, as she strolled into the playroom for the shift she'd been assigned, she noticed two sleeping babies in a cradle by the door. She slipped soundlessly down to the rocking chair beside them, and peered in through the bars of the crib.

The smaller one couldn't have been more than six months old; the other, probably one year or less, was caught in some faraway dream just beyond his twitching little eyes.

"Beautiful, aren't they?"

Sage gave Beth a wistful smile.

"When they're sleeping?" she whispered with a grin. "Yes."

The younger one opened her deep brown eyes and blinked several times before focusing on Sage's face.

"Good afternoon," Sage said softly. "Did you have a nice nap?"

The child instantly reached out for her, which caused Sage to lean back into her chair.

"She wants you," Beth told her. "Go on."

Sage's heart was pounding hard. She hadn't held a baby in years, and then only long enough for an occasional mommy-friend to be satisfied that she was duly envious.

"Oh, no," she said, shaking her head. "I'm supposed to do story time."

"They won't be ready for another fifteen minutes," Beth assured her.

"Still . . ."

When Beth could see that Sage had no intention of acquiescing to the baby's plea, she picked the child up herself. Sage watched as Beth coddled and cooed, rocking gently from one foot to the other, and she slightly envied the enormous smile Beth had been able to bring to the little one's face.

While Beth hummed and spoke to the baby in sing-song assurances over a clean diaper, Sage returned her attention to the sleeping child before her. His pudgy little hands were balled into tight fists, battling some dream-state dragon no doubt, and his toes were curling and uncurling in an indecipherable exercise of the unconscious. Poking her hand through the side of the crib, she ran a finger along the tiny little arm. His skin was hot from sleep, and softer than she could have imagined.

Soft as a baby's bottom, she thought, then smiled. *People pay fortunes for skin like this.*

"I'm going to round up the children," Beth told her, the grinning infant still in her arms. "If Miguel wakes up before I get back, the clean diapers are in the cabinet over there."

Oh, right. I'm going to change his dirty diaper.

Sage watched him cautiously, enthralled with the fringe of fluttering dark lashes resting on his chubby little cheek. Her gaze caressed the sleeping child, from his dark peach-fuzz halo of hair to the dribble stains on the front of his cotton shirt. His little legs were fat and pinkish, and he had a small round birthmark on his flexing ankle.

It stunned Sage when she felt a light touch to her hand, and she darted her eyes toward its source. Miguel had awoken indeed, and he was staring hard at her as if he'd never seen a human being in his short little life. He blinked several times, and then focused on her hand where it had fallen beside him. He took her entire index finger tightly into his fist, then looked back to Sage for permission to borrow it.

"Good morning, sunshine," she smiled, and he returned it, one hundred-fold. "Did you sleep well?"

Miguel held on tightly as Sage shook her finger gently, and she wondered at the odd twinge of amazement that nibbled at her insides.

"I know you probably have a dirty diaper," she whispered as she leaned closer to him. "But if you could just wait until Beth comes back to let us know about it, I'd really appreciate it."

Miguel giggled back at her, and Sage knew she had a co-conspirator in the camp.

"You're aces, Miguel," she told him, then crinkled up her nose and spoke in high-pitched baby talk. "You're the best. Yes, you are. You're the best."

Chapter Five

"Oh, Daddy, I miss you so much. I just want to come home."

"I know, baby," he said, in that special Daddy way he had about him that was one part comforting, two parts all-knowing. "It's just not safe for you until that maniac is behind bars."

"It's so awful here," she confided. "It's dirty and hot, and that overbearing Ben Travis is working me to death like some sort of slave labor."

"Sage, Ben did us an enormous favor by letting you come to Mexico. He didn't have to take that kind of risk, with all those children counting on him. He did it because you needed help."

"Errrgh," she groaned. "He's so arrogant."

Her father's laughter was rich and warm through her cell phone, and it tugged at her bruised heart. How she yearned for one of their afternoons together. A round of golf, and then lemonade on the veranda. She wondered why she hadn't realized how significant those leisurely afternoons really were while she had them in her grasp.

"You'll survive, Sage," he assured her lovingly. "This may end up being a good experience for you."

"Is that why you sent me here? So I'd learn a lesson?"

"No, darling. That's just a perk."

"Oh, thank you, Daddy. Always happy to provide sadistic entertainment for my father."

"Oh, Sage." He softened, and tears instantly rose in her eyes at the mere sound of him speaking her name. "Try to make the best of it. I'll see you again very soon."

"All right, Daddy, I will. I love you."

"I love you, too."

Sage felt a million miles away from her life as she pressed the button and closed off their communication. She wondered about Connie, and the gang down at Firestorm, the dance club she so often frequented. From the flashing light, she could see that her cell phone was almost at the end of an expired battery, and resolved to dig out the charger at some point that day.

The ocean was emerald green that morning, and the sky a vibrant aqua blue, dotted with starched-white clouds. Something caught her eye in the distance, and she turned away from the spectacular view to see a man jogging down the beach toward her.

She knew it was Ben long before he reached her, but she nonchalantly commented, "Oh, it's you," when he ran up.

"What are you doing out so early?" He half-grinned, and the spark in his eye as he leaned over the boulders between them made the air catch in her lungs. He was panting, but it was Sage who had the sudden need for oxygen.

"I needed to make a call," she replied coolly. "There's no privacy anywhere in that camp."

She was immediately sorry for the bit of an attitude in her response when Ben regarded her carefully, one raised brow arched over his intense eyes.

"I'm sorry we can't better accommodate you, your highness," he breathed, then raised himself, preparing to continue his run. "Perhaps you'd like to think about other arrangements. Oh, that's right. You have nowhere else to go."

Now he was the one being snide.

Sage silently watched him continue on down the beach. He was the most maddening man she had ever met.

A man of God! she thought sourly. *HA!*

And yet something inside prodded her. Perhaps in the lack of excitement she'd settled into at the orphanage, she'd found the only thing even close to adventure. She'd found a challenge.

Ben Travis was her challenge. And Sage decided right then and there that she was going to get him to like her, no matter what it took. She wasn't quite sure why it mattered to her so much; he was nothing more than a surfside preacher in a world that could never reach far enough to touch her own, after all. But not knowing why didn't make it matter any less. She was determined to be the recipient of the same smiles and laughs and friendly banter Beth and the others received. She refused to be the outsider, the one he couldn't abide.

Ben Travis, you and I are going to be friends, she vowed.

Ben hadn't gone far when he began chastising himself for his behavior when he'd encountered Sage. She was occupying his private place, after all. That ridge of boulders was his stopping place every day, and something inside him cracked a little when he saw her there. Taking it over. The way she was taking over everything else. Like his thoughts. And the new development. His dreams.

Ben recalled walking into the nursery the previous afternoon, and his heart squeezed as he relived what he'd found there. Sage in the big rocking chair, children gathered around her feet. She was reading the story of Noah's Ark, and, although just a handful of them spoke enough English to glean anything from it, they were enthralled, every one of them looking up at her with wide eyes. Perhaps it was her exquisite beauty that drew their attention so fully, or perhaps the silken tones of her perfect voice, but beneath his aggravation, confusion, irritation, and frustration toward Sage McColl, Ben had to admit that she was indeed fascinating.

In a useless, silver spoon sort of way, he was quick to add, then stepped up the pace of his run. *And I have no patience or time for a spoiled rich kid who will escape this place as soon as she can manage it.*

He added a silent prayer that he would not forget that fact.

It was forced and guarded, even painful, but Ben's apology was at least sincere. Sage admired the fact that he could humble himself enough to make it.

"I apologize," he had managed. "The last thing you need is my sarcasm, and I was wrong. I'm sorry."

She lied when she told him she hadn't given it a second thought; in fact, she'd been awake much of the night before replaying it in her mind, asking herself why he was so bound and determined to dislike her. She recalled his beautiful eyes ablaze with fire as he looked into her, a hostility burning toward her that she just couldn't figure out.

Sage wasn't sure why he'd offered to let her go with him into the nearby town, but she jumped at the chance to get out and see more of the world than the depressing little stretch of beach that housed the saddest array of orphans she could ever have imagined. She grabbed her purse and was in the passenger seat of the pickup truck before Ben had even cranked open his door.

The mirror over the visor was cracked, but she used it anyway to apply a coat of lip gloss, then ran her fingers through waves of fire-red curls.

"It's not New York we're heading for," Ben stated as he turned over the engine, without even looking her way. "It's just Puerto Nuevo."

There it was again. That hostility.

"What is it you dislike about me so much?" she asked him out of the blue after half a dozen long, silent miles.

"Don't be ridiculous," he replied coolly. "I don't know you well enough to dislike you."

Sage watched him for several minutes. He didn't even twitch. He just kept his eyes on the road ahead, as if she weren't even there.

"Is that why you asked me along?" she prodded. "To get to know me well enough to properly dislike me?"

She'd startled him. She could tell by the way his face moved toward her, the way he held her in his sight. And just as quickly, he darted his attention back to the road.

What was it about her that made him so tense?

"I asked you along because I thought you might like a change of scenery," he told her flatly.

"Well, you were right," she finally replied, a grin winding its way over her entire face as she rolled down the window to let the ocean breeze create havoc with her free-flying hair. "And even you cannot ruin this outing for me, Ben Travis."

He stole a look at her just then, her eyes closed, her face boldly positioned into the wind, and a jolt of electricity moved through him. She was the most beautiful woman he'd ever seen.

"Do you suppose there will be shops there?" she asked, throwing him off balance for a moment.

Skimming his attention casually over the road, he nodded. "Yes, there are shops. What are you looking for?"

Sage tucked her head back inside the window and smoothed her tousled hair. "My blue jeans are far too hot and constraining for the work I've been doing. I was hoping to pick up a few pairs of shorts, maybe some T-shirts."

No complaints about scrubbing or peeling or reading to the children. Rather, an adjustment to make her better able to complete the tasks. Now that was surprising.

"I think we can find you something."

Sage saw his reply as a victory. Not a trace of hostility in it. Perhaps she wasn't the only one who had needed a brief change of scenery.

"It's so beautiful," she breathed at the panoramic treasure of white sand and blue ocean.

Yes. You are.

And the alarm bells sounding inside his own heart were not lost on Ben. He knew a train wreck when he met up with one.

Puerto Nuevo was no bigger than a few square miles in each direction. The one main street that ran through its center was littered with shops and street vendors offering souvenir trinkets, local color, and tasty snacks.

Ben turned the pickup unexpectedly down a dirt road, pulling to a dusty stop in the alley.

"What is this place?" Sage asked him, and two locals appeared before he could respond.

Ben climbed from the truck and embraced the men, then slapped them on the backs. They exchanged chatter in Spanish before Ben motioned to Sage to get out and join them.

"This is Sage," he told them. "She's one of our newest volunteers."

The men looked her over carefully, then the more portly of the two smiled and nodded and took her hand to shake it.

Looking Ben in the eye, the man said something in Spanish which obviously pertained to Sage, and then Ben shrugged.

Ben shook his head and smiled, making Sage ask, "What did he say?"

"He said you're too beautiful to be hidden away in Mexico."

Alarm rose in Sage's aquamarine eyes, and she began

to tremble slightly. "How does he know? Have you told him? Is that . . . safe?"

"Relax," he told her softly as the men headed toward the door. Touching her shoulder briefly he added, "He doesn't know. No one outside of camp knows why you're here. They just think you're one of our volunteers."

"Oh. Good."

"Come in and have something cold," Ben's jovial friend invited in broken English, waving them in past the dark burlap curtain that served as a door.

The hallway they followed was narrow and dark, but it emerged into a small cantina decorated with brightly colored tapestries and mirrors in desperate need of cleaning. Waitresses delivered stone plates of beans and rice and seasoned chicken to the patrons dotted about the hodgepodge of tables and chairs, and standard mariachi music played gently in the background.

"Sangria," the jovial one offered, but Ben stopped her before Sage could receive the glass.

"Nothing doing, Juan," he warned his friend good-naturedly. "She'll have the same as me."

Juan shrugged in return, offering Ben two sealed bottles of mineral water, still dripping from their stay in the chest of ice behind the bar.

Sage took the bottle and twisted open the cap, strolling around the cantina to examine the bold mural that occupied all four walls of the tiny place. The colors were audacious and chaotic, the style crudely childlike, but she couldn't help but follow it from wall to wall to wall. When she returned to the bar, Sage noticed Ben talking quietly with a beautiful young Mexican girl, and she hesitated before joining them.

"Sage, this is Maria," he said, and they nodded an amiable greeting. "She's going to take you over to her shop to see if you can find the clothes you were hoping to buy. Here . . ." He paused to open his billfold. "This should be enough."

"I can pay for it myself," she assured him, then chuckled as he showed her the money more carefully. "I'm just too American for my own good." She grinned, then took the pesos from Ben's hand.

"Don't be long," he told her, then muttered something to Maria in Spanish.

Before Sage could thank him for his generosity, Ben had returned his attention to his two friends, and they were already involved in a hushed conversation.

"Maria, do you speak any English?" she asked the girl as she hurried to keep up with her.

She thought Maria had given a short, one-word answer, but she couldn't be certain.

"Because I don't speak more than five words of Spanish," she prattled on, wondering why the girl was in such an extraordinary hurry to take her shopping! "I know some not-so-nice words, I suppose. But high school Spanish left me with little more than asking your name or how you're doing today. And since I know your name is Maria, I guess . . ."

Sage didn't know whether Maria had no interest in engaging in polite conversation or if she was simply deaf to any language besides Spanish, but she thought the girl quite rude as she hurried along the cobblestone sidewalk and quickly disappeared into the doorway of a small shop.

"Oh," Sage shrugged, then followed-the-leader inside.

Colorful cottons, pastel gauzes and woven straw hats made for a lively ambiance in the little place. The chubby old woman behind the counter eyed Sage suspiciously as she moved inside, and Maria shot the woman a nervous smile before muttering several sentences in Spanish.

"I'll just," Sage began, then motioned two fingers walking through the air, "look around. Look around?"

"Sí," Maria nodded, then continued her whispered exchange with the saleswoman.

Sage shrugged it off and began perusing a rack of bold-print skirts. One style in particular caught her eye, a sarong of sorts which tied in a knot at the hip, and she produced two of them in different, vibrant fabrics.

When she saw the two women watching her, hawk-eyed, she raised one of the hangers and smiled. "What do you think? Do you like?"

Maria nodded and forced a tiny smile, but her pudgy companion merely stared a hole right through her.

"I think so," she nodded, trying to remain impervious to the old woman. "I think I like it."

The mirror she stood before was cracked at the corner, and the reflection it produced was foggy. There were no fitting rooms in sight, so Sage decided to improvise, checking the width of the garment against the reflection of her shape in the mirror. It would do, she decided, then moved on to a circular rack that held dozens and dozens of cotton shorts.

A rack bearing straw hats of every shape and size

drew her attention next. Sage didn't know if she'd ever bought a hat out of a real need to be shielded from the glare of the sun; in her world, hats were a fashion tool rather than a necessity. A small one with a rounded, up-turned brim caught her eye and she tried it on. The simple black ribbon around it was tied in a casual bow at the back, and the hat itself fit snugly down low on her head. It would help protect her sensitive skin from the fierceness of the Mexican sun, and she tipped it over the hook of one of the many hangers in her hand and carried her choices up toward the register.

The older woman wasn't even trying to disguise her demeanor any more, and, although Sage didn't know what the woman was saying, she was fully aware that it was being said in regard to her. Furthermore, the pointing of her fat little finger and the tone of her voice confirmed to her that it wasn't good.

"Have I done something wrong?" she asked Maria, as she laid her purchases down on the counter. "Is she angry?"

Maria spat one Spanish word at the woman through gritted teeth, then turned timidly back to Sage.

"I apologize for my aunt," she managed to say in extremely broken English. "She has no like for Americanos." Then, as an afterthought, she added, "Except Señor Ben."

The old woman responded with a "hmmmpph" sound, then turned her nose in the air in Sage's general direction.

"So your aunt knows Ben," Sage commented, then showed the woman her intended purchases and nodded. "Can I pay you for these?"

"Señor Ben very kind to mi familia," Maria told her, then smacked the top of the counter sharply and nodded toward the clothes. Her aunt reluctantly resumed her job.

Maria was helpful in finishing up the transaction, translating the total price for Sage, and helping her figure out what to give the woman from the wad of Mexican pesos she had jammed into her pocket.

When the woman began to speak at ninety miles an hour, Sage looked to Maria for her assistance yet again. She seemed to chastise her aunt briefly in their native tongue, then picked up the plastic bag hugely overstuffed with Sage's purchases and led her toward the front of the shop.

"Juanita raise me mostly," she told Sage, and she was struggling for the English words. "Mi madre die . . . when I am born. She hopes I will one day marry Señor Ben."

Sage stopped just as they left the store, and tugged gently at Maria's arm. The girl was obviously quite embarrassed as she faced her.

"I have no dream," Maria managed to say. "Señor Ben no want young girl when he can be with American woman beautiful like you."

"Oh, Maria," Sage softened. "Ben and I aren't . . . together. We're just friends. Amigos?"

Maria looked at her skeptically.

"Really. We're just friends."

Maria's discomfort softened a bit, and she kicked at the cobblestone with the toe of her worn leather slide-on shoes. "Señor Ben say God will send the right one for him and for me one day. I already find right one. You sent from God for Señor Ben?"

Sage grinned at that. No one had ever accused her of being angelic; at least not in a very long time.

"No," she replied.

"Señor Ben know this?" Maria asked with a raised eyebrow, then set off down the street with Sage's package pressed to her chest with both arms.

Sage remained behind at first, frozen to the spot. Suddenly, the thought of her being sent to Mexico as some divine blessing for Ben Travis fogged her brain. And if that preposterous notion dared somehow be true, even at the edge of her wildest fantasy, would it really be Ben's blessing? Or hers?

Sage shook the thoughts from her head, then jogged off after Maria, who had already reached the front entrance of the cantina. The moment they entered, Maria handed off the package to Sage and was gone again out the front door.

"Wait!" she cried, but it was too late. Maria was hurrying back down the cracked cobblestone. "Thank you," she added, but she knew the girl couldn't hear.

She watched after Maria much longer than she was able to actually see her, then slowly turned back inside the cantina.

"That food smells like heaven," she sighed as she walked up to the barstool beside Ben. "What do I smell?"

"Fresh tortillas," Juan explained with a smile. "Funny thing, all Ben Travis's visits come at tortilla time."

"I'm no idiot," Ben laughed, and Sage reveled in the full, vibrant tone of it. She hadn't had occasion to hear him laugh so unabashedly. It was a beautiful sound, resonating like a lovely old bell chiming somewhere far away. "Why don't we indulge, Sage? What do you say?"

She made a conscious effort to close her mouth and stifle the surprise crackling inside her at the offer. What was at the core of this sudden, casual, even lighthearted, behavior?

"You're asking me to have lunch with you?" She grinned. "Great! I'm starved."

"Bring it on, my friend," he nodded to Juan, placing an arm around Sage's shoulder as he led her to a lumpy leather booth at the corner of the cantina.

"It looks like you found what you were looking for," he observed, as she flopped the large bag down to the seat beside her.

"And how," she smiled. "I'm afraid you don't have much change."

"Keep it," he stated as she reached into her pocket.

Sage cocked her head and stared at Ben, her crooked smile betraying a trace of disbelief.

"What?" he asked, then shifted uncomfortably in his seat.

"Well, who knew?" she exclaimed.

"Who knew what?"

"That all it took to turn you into a normal human being was the promise of a good Mexican meal."

Ben straightened, then looked away momentarily.

"Am I really that bad?" he asked her, and she saw the corner of his mouth twitch slightly as he waited.

Sage released a puff of air and then cringed dramatically.

"Ooohhh," Ben groaned, his hands slapping to his chest as if he'd just been stabbed. "That hurt."

"I could check with Juan," she teased. "I'll bet he has a first-aid kit."

"You're a real gem," he chuckled. "A potato-peeling, diaper-avoiding gem of a human being."

"You knew?" she asked defeatedly.

"That you avoid the babies with dirty diapers? Oh yeah. Everyone knows."

"Hey!" she corrected him with a playful look in her emerald eyes that dared him to challenge her. "But I'll have you know that I could have a very successful career in potato-peeling. Now that I've got the whole idea of it down."

"Not much money in the potato biz though," he noted. "But if that's your calling . . ." He ended the thought with a shrug.

The two of them chuckled as Juan filled the table with plates of fragrant, steaming foods. Chicken and red peppers, onions and tomatoes, beside mounds of reddish rice and pinkish beans.

"What is this?" she asked Juan with a grin.

"Fajitas," he declared.

Ben poked a fork into several of the vegetables, blew on it quickly and devoured it. "That's Spanish for IN-credible," he said.

Sage's first bite confirmed that it was true. And she smiled at her own lighthearted thought.

Okay. Then Ben Travis must be a fajita, too.

Chapter Six

Ben pushed the wire-rimmed sunglasses to their rightful place upon his nose as he turned over the engine of the old pickup. When he turned to check the alley before backing out, he hoped that Sage wasn't aware of just how long his gaze had lingered on her.

"I can't . . . seem to . . ." she mumbled. He noticed that she was struggling with her seat belt, so he tossed the gearshift back into Park and leaned over to lend a hand.

"It's an old truck," he said as he took the buckle from her. "It's just a little . . ." The belt clicked into place, and he smiled. ". . . temperamental."

"I can understand that," she replied softly, their eyes locking for several long moments.

When Ben broke the connection, it was not without cost. He felt it as keenly as if he were a wall being scraped of all its old layers of paint. Neither of them spoke for a while, and he tried not to take notice of the dance her long red hair was doing from the force of a mild ocean breeze through her fully open window.

Ben wondered once again what it was about Sage that set his teeth to grinding at some times, and diverse emotions into gear at others. She was clearly not a woman he would normally be attracted to (on any level besides the physical, of course), and yet he had to admit, even just to himself, that there had been days since he met her when he'd found himself thinking of future days filled with her presence.

She is going to be gone soon, he reminded himself fiercely. *Don't go getting tangled up in her life and forget that.*

He noticed, out of the corner of his eye, that Sage had produced a pair of Ray-Bans from the small purse she carried. He willed himself not to look as she put them on, then pulled a straw hat from the puffed bag of purchases and placed it low on her forehead. It only took him an instant to break that will, and he found himself doing battle against a thousand adversaries when his vision rested on her.

Face upturned to the wind, eyes seemingly closed behind the dark glasses, she held the hat down with one hand while the other extended out the window and played with the rushing wind. Posed much like she had been on the ride out to Puerto Nuevo, her natural beauty struck Ben like a sucker punch to his gut, and it was sheer torture to drag his gaze back to the road.

"I had fun today," she told him when they'd pulled into camp and parked the truck. "I really did."

Before Ben could reply, Sage moved toward him, and,

with a gentle hand on his shoulder for balance, planted a quick little kiss on his cheek.

"Thank you."

"You're welcome," he managed in a raspy voice. Then, as an afterthought, he added, "Now off with you. There are diapers to be changed."

Sage erupted into a fit of giggles, then headed into the camp, walking backwards to face him. "Diapers? Oh, uh, I've got potato duty, I think. Can't talk. Gotta run."

He watched her trot up the incline of the clay hill. At the top, several children greeted her with warm smiles and embraces. His heart fluttered as her lyrical laughter echoed back to him, and then again as she took the hat from her head and placed it on Coco's as they walked.

It hadn't even been two weeks, and yet Sage McColl seemed a perfect fit in this world. Despite that part of her which was spoiled, over-indulged, and self-involved . . . there was also something there Ben hadn't imagined. A softness lingered beneath her facade, a desire to be accepted for who and what she was. And something else as well. An inner strength, he supposed. That special something that allowed her to find joy in even the most unusual circumstances, like the kiss of wind on her face, or the sight of the ocean at midday.

When Sage had first come to the orphanage, Ben had held out very little hope that she would adjust. But adjust she had! And now, he reluctantly admitted, she was as much a part of things as he or Beth or the children were. At least in his mind.

And in my heart, he added, then immediately chastised himself.

* * *

Miguel was instantly enthralled by the sound of the tiny wooden maraca Sage had brought from Juan's cantina. She knew he would love it; it was like a rattle just slightly too big for his tiny hand.

As she leaned over the crib and lifted the infant out of it, Sage recalled how reluctant she had been to hold him when she'd first arrived. But he'd slipped quietly into her heart day after day until, with the outstretched arms she had come to love so dearly, she answered him with an unconscious and natural reciprocation. And now . . . now, Sage couldn't imagine a life without this baby in her arms, without a whole fist clasped firmly around one solitary finger, without the shining laughter or heart-wrenching tears of this one little boy.

Oh, she loved the others too, there was no doubt. But something about Miguel called out to her in a way she had never known or dreamed. Something inside his eyes connected with something inside hers and, although she knew she could never explain it in words, they were undoubtedly bonded by something far more deep. It was the closest thing to maternal emotions that she thought she could ever feel, and she didn't know whether to revel in them or run away as fast as she could.

Sage lowered herself into the old wooden rocker near the window, and Miguel curled himself over her shoulder. Holding tight to one thick lock of her hair, he snuggled into the crook of her neck while she hummed softly and traced circles on his tiny back. The moment was a revelation for Sage: a quiet, peaceful revelation broken only by the emerging warmth to her arm where it rested beneath Miguel's behind.

"Ohhh, Miguel," she groaned. "Honey . . ."

Reluctantly checking, she realized it was indeed the disaster she had dreaded. She'd relaxed him to the point that he'd soiled his diaper. And without another person in sight to whom she could hand the baby over.

"You little stinker," she said, crinkling her nose at the increasing odor. "And I mean that. You stink!"

"That's my cue." Beth's smiling face caught Sage by surprise as she moved toward her with outstretched arms. "I'll take care of him."

"No," Sage objected, then questioned her own voice. "Show me how."

Beth raised a skeptical brow and then grinned from ear to ear. "Okay, honey," she slowly nodded. "Step up to the changing table."

Sage nearly lost her lunch several times during the ordeal, but she survived, and a smiling Miguel rewarded her for it by stretching out his arms to her and cooing softly. She lifted him to her and kissed the top of his head playfully several times, then cradled him to her chest, rocking gently from one foot to the other.

"You look quite at home with that baby in your arms," Beth told her, and she thought she saw a mist of tears in the woman's eyes before she blinked it away.

"Miguel is a very good teacher," Sage told her, snuggling her cheek against his.

"Oh, Sage." Beth smoothed the hair around Sage's face and smiled sweetly. "If only your mother could see you this way. She would be so proud."

"You think so?" Sage asked, and she wondered at the thought of it.

"I know so. And your father . . ."

"Daddy?" Sage chuckled. "Daddy would faint dead away."

"You might be right," Beth replied, and they shared a good-natured laugh at his expense.

Sage walked into the empty mess hall just in time to hear Ben's familiar voice groan in obvious frustration.

"If they turn us down, we'll be out of business, Beth," he said urgently. "It will shut us down completely."

Beth cleared her throat softly, and she and Ben and one of the other volunteers—Larry, Sage recalled—turned around to face her. She felt conspicuous standing there with an empty baby bottle, all of them staring at her that way.

"I was just going to get some milk," she told them, then displayed the bottle. "I didn't mean to interrupt."

"Don't be silly, honey," Beth said as she headed toward her with a warm smile. "Let's get that bottle filled."

Sage allowed Beth to lead her toward the kitchen, both men silent as she passed, Ben with his eyes lowered to the ground.

"What's going on?" she whispered when they were out of earshot. "Has something happened?"

"It's orphanage business," Beth replied, then set about filling the bottle with powdered milk and water from a plastic jug. "It can be very frustrating."

"What is it?" she persisted. "Why is Ben so upset?"

Beth sighed, conceding. "You've obviously noticed that our situation here is crude at best." Sage half-shrugged in agreement. "Right now, we get our water from town."

"Juan's cantina, right?" Sage asked. "I saw the delivery on my first week here. Has Juan changed his mind?"

"No, no, he would never do that. He's loyal to the work we do here, through and through. But the authorities don't take kindly to the arrangement; they say there are health issues, regulations." Beth waved her hand and rolled her eyes slightly as if to say they were idiots. "And they tell us that, in order to continue operations here, we must be hooked into the city's water supply officially."

"Well, that sounds like progress," Sage suggested. "Then we'll have actual running water here in camp."

"Except that it's going to cost somewhere in the neighborhood of seventy-five thousand American dollars to set it up. Plus the monthly bills that are now being absorbed by Juan out of the goodness of his heart. And the Mexican authorities have no intention of assisting Americans in taking up residence in their country. Ben thinks they're cooking this up just so they can get us to move on."

"But what about the children?" she asked. "What will happen to them?"

"That question echoes in my head morning and night."

They both looked up to find Ben standing in the doorway, his hair disheveled and his face careworn, weary.

"Ben, I'm sorry. She could see that something was wrong."

He waved his hand at Beth, dismissing her concern. "It was going to come out soon anyway." He tried to smile, then looked at Sage seriously. "They've given us a deadline of the end of the month, and every avenue we've tried has been a dead end. There is no one in this country willing to help, despite the fact that these children are their own. They're Mexican children. There simply is not enough money or time to meet their requirements, and the government forbids us to take the children across the border to care for them there under U.S. guidelines for aid."

"What about finding homes for them?" she suggested half-heartedly.

"If there were homes for these children here in Mexico," Beth explained, "there would be no need for us to be here to begin with. We are all they have."

"And what would it take to get the government to change their mind? To get the children across the border to America?"

"A miracle." Ben sighed. "A big, bright and shining miracle."

"Well, isn't that your area?" Sage asked innocently.

Ben and Beth looked at one another and smiled knowingly.

Beth chuckled, then placed an arm around Sage's shoulders. "Let's go get that milk to its baby."

Sage looked back at Ben before heading out alongside Beth. She remembered his hushed conversation with Juan the day they'd gone to town, and his almost-euphoric mood that followed. He must have thought there was hope at that point, and the contrast between now and then was severe and sad.

"I wish there was something I could do," she told Beth as they walked across the camp, and she meant it with all her heart.

"I know you do."

"What if I called Daddy? Asked him for the money."

"Even if he wired the money tomorrow," Beth said,

sighing, "there wouldn't be enough time to make the arrangements."

"Surely if Ben talks to the authorities, explains . . ."

"They set down these demands knowing full well we could never meet them," Beth replied. "They're not about to make any special exceptions now. Believe me; Ben has tried."

"He looks so beaten," Sage thought out loud. "So sad."

"This is his life's work. Remember, he and his wife built this place when there were only twelve children to house. Mexico is a very poor country in this region, and the number of children grew in no time at all. The one thing that Ben has always done, though, is open the door to the next child in need of shelter. He has never turned a child away."

"Does anyone ever come to help?" Sage asked.

"Twice a year, church groups come from the United States," Beth began, then wiped the perspiration from her brow with the back of her shirtsleeve. "They meet the children, they spend a day or a week, and they donate their time and money to upgrade the camp. It's no luxury hotel, but it's in far less disrepair than it was in the beginning, or even just a few years ago."

"Don't any of those people show any interest in adopting the children?" Sage asked incredulously. "I can't imagine meeting them and not being changed."

"We've adopted a few out to good homes," Beth explained. "Four, maybe five children per year. But those have been families who came down to help, and the red tape involved in getting the children placed into American homes is beyond belief. You have no idea . . ."

No, I guess I don't, she admitted to herself, then took Beth's hand into hers.

"Don't give up," Sage encouraged her. "Ben will think of something. I know he will."

Chapter Seven

"There has to be something you can do, Daddy," Sage said frantically into her cell phone. "We can't just let this happen. If you could see these children; if you only knew . . ."

"I'll try, darling," he assured her. "I'll call Rafe just as soon as we hang up and see if there's some sort of intervention we can arrange. But don't get your hopes up, Sage."

"I have to," she said softly, wiping away the fog of emotion from her eyes as her vision rested on Miguel, smiling in his crib. "I have to hope."

"That Detective Martin has been around nearly every day," Mac told her, changing the subject.

"Who?" she asked.

"Ray Martin," he replied.

"Oh," she nodded, remembering his dark good looks and deceivingly friendly smile.

"He's quite insistent about finding you."

"Why does he want to find me so badly?" she asked.

"He says it's to assure himself that you're protected," her father said softly. "But I can't take that chance."

"But, Daddy, maybe I should come back. Let them use me to draw Eric out. Then at least this whole ordeal would be over."

"But how will it end?" he asked her. "And when? I want you far away and safe until it does."

"I appreciate that, but . . ."

"There will be no more talk of you coming home. Not until Eric Randolph is behind bars."

She set the phone down on the counter and moved toward the baby, who was happily engaged in discovering the nuances of his own toes. When he sensed that she was near, Miguel looked up and grinned from ear to ear, then raised his arms toward her.

"Hi, sweetness," she cooed at him as she lifted him to her, and he smacked her cheek firmly with open palms.

"Ma . . . ma," he told her matter-of-factly, then patted her face once more.

"I love you, too," she told him emotionally, then began to cry.

Miguel seemed curious about her tears, and he began rubbing them over her cheeks. Sage closed her eyes tight and felt the smooth silk of his hand massage the moisture into her face, then she kissed him on the top of the head.

"I miss my home so much," she whispered to the baby. "I can't even begin to imagine what it's like for you."

"Ma," he croaked, and they shared a smile that squeezed at Sage's heart.

She set him down in the nearby playpen, where he happily clunked blocks upon other blocks as she made her rounds to check on the other children, still sleeping. They were all ages and shapes of babies, each of them beautiful in their own unique way. The thought of turning them out to homelessness was something Sage was not capable of considering.

Anyway, Ben would never let that happen.

Miguel's sudden wail of exasperation drew her attention immediately, and she saw that two of his beloved blocks had landed on the ground outside the playpen. She picked them up and returned them, but the child had lost interest in anything besides her presence. He held out his arms to her sweetly and pouted, saying "Ma," before breaking into unexplained sobs.

Sage picked him up and held him close to her.

"I don't like babies much," she teased him in a high-pitched voice which drew his undivided attention. "But I sure do like you."

The tiny little boy cocked his head slightly and stared at her intensely, as if he were struggling to decipher her words. Perhaps he was able to read her thoughts, she wondered. Able to feel the loss she was drowning in. She'd come to this place against her will, and when the time came she would leave it the same way.

She remembered the first day she had set foot in the nursery. Remembered how she had never lamented not being able to have children . . . until just lately. The charm of the children was most irresistible, and they had changed her.

For the better, she hoped.

And Ben had changed her as well. Just knowing him, standing in the light of his dedication to these little ones, had been a revelation, even before she'd been able to find something about him to love.

Love. Where did that come from? She didn't love Ben Travis, for heaven's sake!

And at that very moment, Miguel clinging to her as he wailed, Sage realized that it might never be possible for her to return to her old life, her old ways.

"Shhhh," she soothed, rubbing the peach-fuzz hair on his little head. "Shhhhh, everything's going to be all right." And when he sniffled slightly and began to calm down, Sage instinctively began to sing to him softly.

"Amazing grace . . . how sweet the sound . . ."

Miguel lifted his eyes to hers, entranced by the sound of her voice.

"I once was lost . . . but now I'm found . . . was blind, but now I see."

"I think you've got him under your spell," Beth whispered, and Sage looked up to find her and Ben standing in the doorway.

She flushed slightly when she saw them, and she noticed something akin to surprise in Ben's tired blue eyes. Or was she imagining it?

"Your mother used to sing that song to you," Beth recalled, and she reached up to smooth the hair away from Sage's face.

"She did? I don't remember." Sage tried to smile, but it came across as a weary attempt.

She ached to say something that would bring back the

hope in Ben, that would elicit that same bright, beautiful laughter she'd discovered in Puerto Nuevo. She wanted to tell him about her conversation with her father, how hard she believed that he would do something to fix things the way he always had throughout her life. But she wouldn't.

She would wait until she had something definite to tell. If she was indeed sentenced to spend her time in a foreign country, changing dirty diapers and living without warm baths, manicures or mud facials, she could at least make the best of the time spent there. So, in the meantime, she would hope *for* Ben. Hope in the efforts of her strong and wonderful father, hope in his past victories and the certain results he had always been able to command. She would hope that there was something he would be able to do to save this insignificant little orphanage.

It dawned on Sage just then how much time had passed since she had told her father what a wonderful man she thought he was.

Had she ever told him?

Sage vowed then that, if she hadn't, their next conversation would right that wrong.

When he opened his eyes, Ben thought that the view from atop his boulder reflected his own weariness. The usual morning sunlight peered shyly from behind a haze of milky clouds, and the tide seemed to lap lazily to and fro.

After all these years, is it over?
And, if so, what will become of the children?

A brief thought of Laura tickled the innermost part of his heart. The work at the orphanage had been set into motion by her initially. It was only later that Ben had been drawn to the cause, and, by the time they'd learned of the cancer silently eating away at her, his commitment had advanced as well. Laura's dying breath had been spent on thoughts for the welfare of those kids, and Ben had promised her to carry on the work. But now . . .

Their laughter announced the children's arrival before he actually saw them bound over the top of the hill. His heart raced slightly as Sage came into view, Coco's little hand in hers, and a long chain of children whipping down the embankment behind them. Her laughter harmonized with theirs, and Ben's heart leapt with joy at the sight of her.

How she had changed in the short time since she had arrived in Mexico! Ben recalled that first night in the mess hall. She'd been a fish out of water in every way, as far removed from her surroundings as anyone ever could have been. Biding her time, just waiting out the crisis which had propelled her into his world. Just waiting to go home.

Ben watched her now, her long skirt hiked up above her knees, jumping and using her bare feet to create retaliatory splashes out of the puddles of salt water left behind by the last wave that had kissed the shore. She seemed so much in her element with the children now, and Ben smiled at the memory of their first meeting in the wee hours in her San Diego kitchen. He could hardly believe this was the same girl.

She had been somewhat of a siren back then as she

tiptoed across the floor, her shoes swinging from her bright coral fingertips. She'd spilled orange juice on the floor, and would have been completely content to leave it there for someone else to clean up. And now . . . Now, she struck him as three parts woman and one part child, totally at ease with herself and her obscure surroundings, and gleeful, even joyous.

It dawned on him that Sage possessed a certain quality of adaptability he hadn't given her credit for when it was first suggested that she seek refuge there with them. She apparently possessed an unusual ability to adapt quickly to any surroundings. And with that realization came the subsequent reminder that one day soon, Sage McColl would go back to her old life, to her home and her night-life and her array of friends, where she would quickly fit in once again as if she'd never left it all behind. There would likely be little more than a blip on the screen of her adjustment meter, Ben admitted, and he and the children would soon be long forgotten.

Ben wasn't quite comfortable with the alarm that coursed through him at the thought.

"Hi!" Sage beamed, appearing before him as if on cue.

"Where's Beth?" he asked.

"We switched today," she told him. "I think her back is bothering her again."

Beth had struggled with the pain in her lower back more and more recently, and Ben couldn't help but worry. That had been Laura's first sign of impending disaster, after all. Just simple back pain left unattended for far too long. Until it grew into something more se-rious, more heinous. And then . . .

"So I get to play with the big kids," Sage joked. "Wanna join us and get wet? Or shall I round them up for services?"

"By all means," he replied, shaking his thoughts away from the grim past. "Let's get things started."

Sage scurried off obediently, calling out to the children.

She hollered, "Gather around!" in Spanish through arched hands pressed around her mouth, and Ben shook his head again, this time with a grin.

When did she learn to speak Spanish?

Everything about Sage these days amazed Ben in some way. Her easy way with the kids; the way she looked when the breeze feathered through those long red curls. And especially the melody of her voice when he'd happened upon her in the nursery the day before.

Ben's grandmother used to say that the true test of a person down into their soul was what they were like with a child when they thought no one else was looking. If that were truly the test of who Sage was, Ben feared he might never break free of the spell.

He'd heard "Amazing Grace" in his dreams that night, and in the dark distance as he'd struggled with sleep. Ben felt certain that it had been the most beautiful sight he'd ever witnessed, Sage with a toddler's cheek to hers, singing softly. He was also certain that the vision would haunt him long after Sage had left him far behind.

Sage called out to the children again as she joined them, and Ben watched her guide each little body into place, then take her own position beside them as Ben hopped down and jogged across the sand.

"Good morning!" he greeted them, with as sunny a smile as he could muster.

"Buenos dias, Señor Ben," they sang, and the untainted joy in the eyes of those children lifted Ben to an instant state of reciprocity.

Chapter Eight

Sage thought she'd gotten pretty good after only a couple of weeks' time. She could almost understand the message Ben preached in Spanish. If she concentrated very hard, little flashes of recognition built a train of recognizable phrases that went clickety-clack through her brain. But she had to focus most intensely.

Her mind had begun to wander a few minutes in, and she was drawn back long enough to join in their circle of prayer, taking great relish in the tiny hands in both of hers. She couldn't quite make out specifically what Ben was praying for, but she had every confidence in its importance. With every head bowed, and all eyes closed including hers, Ben's beautiful voice caressed her soul just as the ocean breeze tickled her face.

Ben approached her, smiling, when the group had broken up.

"Shall we check on Beth?" he asked her, but Larry chimed in.

"Gail just headed up that way."

The children had already scattered, and the three adults made their way slowly up the beach toward camp.

"Sage, what do you hear from home?" Larry inquired casually.

Knowing that Larry might not be fully aware of the details of her situation, she took an equally casual stance and smiled. "Not too much."

"So how long will you stay with us?"

"Sage isn't sure how long," Ben interjected. "But we're thankful for every day she gives us."

"That reminds me, I haven't heard back from my father," she commented as they reached the clearing. "I've called several times and can't catch him, even on his cell phone."

"Did you leave a message?" Larry asked her innocently.

"Um, no."

How could she explain that even just a voice mail message was suspect, that it could be intercepted? At times, she had been able to lose herself in Ben's world of children and camp life, but the underlying reminder that Eric was still out there, probably hunting her like an animal at that very moment, was never fully forgotten.

"Why don't you try him again now," Ben suggested, and Sage nodded in response.

"Just as soon as I check on Beth."

About the time the threesome reached the nursery,

Larry's wife, Gail, hurried out of the doorway and up to Sage.

Taking her hand, she earnestly said, "Beth needs to see you right away."

"Is she all right?" Larry asked, and Gail motioned him back as Sage and Ben burst inside.

"Beth?"

Sage's heart pounded furiously in her chest, and her palms turned instantly to ice.

"Beth? What is it?" Ben asked cautiously, and the woman lifted her eyes to reveal a well of standing tears.

"Beth, you're scaring us," Sage added, and an iron anchor began to sink inside her.

"It's Mac, honey. He's been shot."

It took a great deal of effort for Sage to focus on what was being said over the roar of her own blood pounding in her ears. She felt dizzy, and her heart ached in a very physical way.

"Daddy's been shot?"

". . . said that Eric was desperate, and he knew Mac would be the only road to find you . . . at St. John's Hospital . . . critical condition . . . comatose . . ."

"What?" She stopped her. "He's in a coma?"

"I think you'd better sit down," Ben said, and then he led her to the rocking chair. She lowered herself to it, but was thoroughly unaware of it.

"I have to go home," she stated matter-of-factly, focusing on nothing in particular before her. "I have to be with my father."

"That's much too dangerous," Ben objected. "You

can't just walk right into the hospital. Randolph will be waiting . . ."

As his words began to sink in, Sage felt a fire rising inside her.

"My father has been shot!" she seethed, and her visual clarity began to sharpen into focus. "I'm going to be with him."

"Look, Sage, I know you love your father," Ben began, but she interrupted him as she flew from the chair.

"Listen to me, Ben Travis!" she cried. "My father is in that coma because of me. If I have to square off with Eric face-to-face, then I will do that! But I *will not* be kept from my father's side."

"No one's suggesting . . ." he attempted.

"Well, it's a good thing," she spat. "Because there is no one and nothing that could keep me from going back to San Diego to be with him. Do you understand?"

Ben groaned as he turned away, biting his lip. To halt the explosion in his eyes from proceeding into words, no doubt. Sage felt the tiniest twinge of guilt for raging at him, but she drowned the life from it with very little effort.

"Sage," he managed to say, calmly. "Isn't there someone there we can call? One of the police officers on the case."

"No!" she sighed, exasperated. "I'm going home, whether you take me or I take myself."

"Sage," Beth spoke up for the first time. "Of course you want to be with your dad. And you will be."

"That's right, I will," she added defiantly.

"We just have to take some time to work it out so that you can do so while still protecting yourself."

Sage considered Beth's logic.

"Calm down, honey, and you'll know I'm right."

Sage looked to Ben and their eyes locked. She knew he noticed the softening vulnerability there when he sighed and then moved toward her.

"You being safe was so important to Mac," he told her as he held her with both hands planted firmly on her shoulders, "that he put himself into jeopardy to protect you. Let's consider that and be wise in our next move."

Sage nodded and, as Miguel began to cry, she was aware for the first time of her surroundings.

"Okay, tiny man," Beth soothed, as she lifted him into her arms. "Okay."

Sage looked up into Ben's eyes, and at the endless chains of unspoken emotions that kindled there. Finally, he graced her with a comforting smile and took her gently into his arms.

"Don't worry," he whispered as he delicately kissed her hair. Sage slowly wound her arms around his neck and held on tight as the tears began to fall.

Sage's words turned over and over in Ben's mind that night as he tried to grab hold of sleep. He made a decision during his sleeplessness, and he followed through just after dawn the next morning by calling together the leadership at the orphanage. Over morning coffee, while all the children remained asleep, they began to formulate a plan.

Ben would bring Maria in from town to help Larry and Gail keep things running smoothly for the kids. That was one priority he wasn't going to allow to get lost in this whole mess.

He gave Larry and Gail a brief overview of Sage's situation, then discouraged their many questions in an effort to save time.

"Beth," he said directly. "It would only be natural for you to rush to the side of your friend as soon as you heard. You'll be our eyes and ears. You'll go to Mac's side, gather the information, and bring it back to Sage and me at the hotel."

"I want to see him with my own eyes, Ben," Sage objected. "Can't you understand that?"

"Of course I can," he replied. "Hear me out."

She gently surrendered with a nod. "I'm sorry."

"Beth will spend a day or so at the hospitals . . ."

"A day or so? What if he . . . he . . . What if he doesn't have a day or so, Ben?"

"We have to find out what the schedule is in order to get you into his room without anyone knowing you're there," he reasoned, then silently prayed she would understand the logic.

"All right then," he said when no one had anything to add. "We'll head out around 7:00."

When Larry and Gail went off to check on the children, and Sage set out to pack a few things for the trip, Ben heaved a deep sigh and planted himself atop the toy chest beside Beth.

"She's a headstrong girl," he said as if Beth hadn't already known.

"Yes, she is." The woman grinned. "And she adores her father."

"This is quite a mess, isn't it, Beth? What kind of choices does a woman have to make for such chaos to fall into her life?"

"Now you know better than that," she said sweetly. "Choices or no choices, sometimes there's just no explaining tragedy."

Ben knew that she was right. In his head, at least. But in his heart . . . well, that was another matter entirely.

Chapter Nine

A golden ball of sunlight collapsed behind the edge of the horizon just as the pickup truck pulled into line at the California border. Uniformed tough-guys with the stereotypical look of United States Marines manned three stopping points, inspecting the insides of every car before letting it pass.

Sage's heart rattled inside her, and she positioned the straw hat just a little lower on her head. It was unnecessary, of course. She'd done nothing wrong, no one was looking for her besides Eric, and they weren't going to give her a hard time about re-entering her own country, but acid churned in her stomach just the same until well after Ben was waved across the boundary at last.

Too many spies-sneaking-across-the-border movies, she supposed. *Those were Daddy's favorite kind.*

Sage's heart winced at the thought of him. She could almost see him there, his lovely tanned face paled with sleep, and his gray-blue eyes clamped helplessly shut. Oh, how she longed to be there beside him. Perhaps if she talked to him . . . if he heard her voice . . .

She instantly banished the burgeoning thought that it might already be too late.

Ben looked into the back seat and smiled at Beth, who was positioned sideways, asleep, with her head resting on the back of the seat.

"She's beat," he said softly to Sage.

"Do you think we can get her to see a doctor while we're here?" she asked in return. "I'm very worried about her back."

Ben's face paled, and Sage touched his hand. "Did I say something wrong?"

"No," he answered. "No."

"What is it?"

"My wife died of uterine cancer," he revealed. "The only sign we ever had was the back pain she suffered."

Sage looked back at Beth momentarily, then squeezed Ben's hand.

"Every time a woman strains her back, my instincts kick in."

"And it takes you back," she said knowingly. "I understand."

"Let's do try and work in a doctor's visit." He smiled after a time. "Maybe get her some muscle relaxants, to help ease the pain."

Sage nodded, then faced straight ahead. She didn't want to remove her hand from over his; there was such a comfort in his touch. Ben must have been thinking the same thing, she realized, when he turned his hand over and laced his fingers with hers.

With a slight squeeze, Ben let their clasped hands rest on the seat between them, and Sage's senses reeled at the simple pleasure of it.

Sage pushed herself up from the chair and began to pace in front of the window once again.

"Does that help?" Ben asked, semi-seriously. "Does your pacing do anything at all to bring Beth back to this room even one minute faster?"

"It does something for me," she replied, straight-faced. "So leave me alone."

Beth had been gone more than two hours, and St. John's Hospital was only ten minutes from their little motel. Sage and Ben had decided to wait together in the women's room because it was much bigger than Ben's single one, but there still didn't seem to be enough room for the two of them.

"What could be taking her so long?" Sage repeated for the dozenth time. "Do you think she's all right?"

"She's perfectly safe, Sage. Stop worrying."

She shot him a glare before plopping down in the chair once more. With a sigh, she began to flip through the *People* magazine on the table without really seeing what was printed on the pages. When the pickup finally pulled up outside the window, Sage and Ben nearly ran into one another to get to the door.

Beth was holding her back as she limped slightly on her path into the room.

"How is he?" Sage demanded the moment she flung the door open.

"He's holding his own," she replied, stepping in and making a beeline for the table and chairs. "He's still in a coma, but they say his vital signs are strong and there's a very good chance he could come out of it."

"Beth," Ben said as he stood over her and took her hand, "you're white as a ghost. Are you all right?"

Sage was ashamed that she hadn't noticed. Beth really did look completely and utterly spent.

"Oh, it's just my back," she told him. "It has a mind of its own."

Sage and Ben exchanged quick glances before Ben said, "Okay, tell us more about Mac."

"That's really all there is to tell about him," she said. "But we've got bigger fish to fry, that's for sure."

"Explain?" Ben commented.

"Well, I met that Detective Martin while I was there," she began, then paused to pour a glass of water from the plastic pitcher on the table. "It seems that, after Mac was shot, just before he slipped into the coma, he called out Sage's name."

"My name?" she asked, then took Ben's offered hand.

"The officers investigating the case thought he might be providing the name of his assailant," she told them disapprovingly. "The good detective says he's very well aware that Sage was not the one who pulled the trigger."

"And did he tell them that?" she urged.

"No. He told me he's not going to discourage them in any way from finding you and pulling you in, even if it means you're wanted for the attempted murder of your own father for that to happen."

"This is . . . absurd!!" Sage cried, catapulting to her feet. "Ben, I could never do something like that to my own father. To anyone! But especially not to Daddy."

"Martin is well aware of that," Beth sympathized.

"Daddy put himself into the line of fire because of me," Sage seemed to think aloud. "He wanted me to be protected."

"But he forgot to worry about who would be policing him," Ben added.

"Don't you dare blame my father for this," she said softly, her eyes fixed on a stain on the carpeted floor. "It's my fault, not his."

"There's no place for laying blame," he assured her. "But we've got to start doing things the right way."

"Like what?" she asked finally, after several minutes of silence.

"I think you should let me call that detective," he suggested. "Talk things over with him."

"No."

"Sage."

"No."

Their eyes locked for an eternity, his insistence pressing in on her stubborn disposition.

"No, she said, after a long moment had passed. "*I'll* call him. After I've seen my father."

The parking lot outside the hospital was eerily still beneath the yellow glow of the overhead lights. Ben and Sage had left Beth behind at the hotel, and Sage could hardly contain herself until she could reach Mac's side. He needed to know she had come. That she was safe. That she loved him.

"Careful," Ben warned as they slipped through the electronic glass doors that granted them entry to a silent ER.

The clock on the stark-white wall behind the nurse's

station read 1:17 A.M., and Sage gratefully trotted past the desk before the lone nurse on duty could turn around. Her large, cumbersome shape also made her miss the entry of Ben, who had hustled through behind Sage.

"There," Sage whispered, but Ben didn't hear her. "Be-en," she stressed softly, then pulled him by the arm and nodded sideways. "The elevator."

Ben grinned as he followed her lead. He pushed the button several times before the door slid shut.

"Well, aren't you just as cool as a cucumber," he teased.

"All those years of sneaking into the house after curfew," she stated seriously. "I knew it would come in handy for something."

"Practice makes perfect, McColl."

The lilt in his voice sent a warm shudder up Sage's spine. If there weren't so very much at stake, she might actually be enjoying herself.

"Oh, God, please," she whispered as the car came to a stop. "Don't let there be anyone around."

"Amen," Ben added carelessly.

Sage was the first to emerge when the doors slid open. She took a quick look in both directions, then gave Ben a thumbs-up. The twosome galloped down the hall, reading the signs indicating room numbers as they went. Sage took Ben's hand in hers for a moment as she focused in on the door, just another few yards away from where they stood.

"Be careful," he warned. "Check inside first."

They cautiously moved into the darkened room, and the adrenaline pumping inside her from the shared adventure with Ben transformed into warm, liquid worry for her father. She moved closer to the bed, taking careful, steady steps forward.

"Daddy."

His face was ashen, and his hand in hers was as cold as ice. Sage looked over the electronics above his bed, and countered his heartbeat double-time with her own.

"I'm so sorry," she whispered to him, and hot tears began to amble down her ivory face. "Oh . . . Ben . . ."

He was at her side in an instant, both of his arms around her, pressing her into the full support of his body. It felt warm and safe there next to him, the warmth of his body creating an aura of protection that she couldn't quite explain. Her father had always been her protector, she realized. Then she looked down at the lifeless shell that was left.

"Daddy, I'm here," she told him once she'd begun to find her calm. "I love you so much."

"He knows, Sage," Ben encouraged her. "He really does."

"No," she argued, sounding very much like a frantic child. "He might not, Ben. I've never told him how . . . how . . . extraordinary I think he is. And now I might never get . . . the . . . chance."

"It makes you want to do everything in your power to honor your father's wishes so that the police can catch the man who did this, doesn't it, Ms. McColl?"

Ben and Sage both reeled to find Detective Martin behind them in the dark shadows of the room. Even in low light, his eyes glimmered with the sparkle of someone other than an ordinary police detective.

"I figured you'd show up here eventually," he told her in earnest.

"Ben," Sage gasped, and he took her hand into his and patted the top of it lovingly.

"Detective Ray Martin," he said as he emerged, his hand outstretched toward Ben.

"Ben Travis," Ben replied, then shook the man's hand.

"I'm happy to see you're still in one piece, Ms. McColl," the detective offered, but she tossed her nose into the air and turned away from him.

"I'm sure you've been up nights worrying," she said sarcastically. "If you would have been protecting me as effectively as you protected my father, I'd be dead by now."

"Your father stashed you away and willingly stepped into your path with no permission from me," he reasoned. "I don't agree with his method, but his motives I can certainly understand."

Sage released a puff of air and coldly stared him down.

Raymond Martin wasn't a bad-looking man, she admitted to herself. He did have nice eyes. Not the eyes of a policeman, but the eyes of a brother, or a doctor, someone you could trust. But beautiful eyes and a killer smile weren't enough to pull the wool over Sage's eyes!

"Is that why you let people think I might have been the one who shot my father?" she asked haughtily.

"If I thought it would keep you from getting yourself killed," he said without wavering, "I would arrest you right here and now. You could be sitting in a jail cell until we can get this whole thing sorted out."

"You can't do that!" she cried.

"I can pretty much do anything I want," he said honestly. "And what I want is to round up Randolph and close this case without another human being paying the price."

"Well, what I want . . ." Sage shouted, and the simple touch of Ben's hand to her arm caused her to soften in an instant. "I just want . . . to see my father," she pleaded. "Can I just have ten minutes alone with him?"

"And then?" he asked her.

"And then," she began, then looked to Ben. "Then . . . we'll talk."

Ben gave her shoulder a squeeze before walking out of the room ahead of Ray.

"She's scared," she heard Ben say as the door closed behind them.

"She has every right to be," Martin replied.

Chapter Ten

"I don't know if I could convince her to go back even if I wanted to try," Ben said thoughtfully, his hip resting against the plastic wall guard in the corridor. "This turn of events with her father has changed everything."

"Her father is the very soul who would want her to go back," Ray reasoned. "The whole thing was his idea. I was never in favor of it. Never. But now . . . I do wonder . . . if maybe he had the right idea. If that's the only way we can protect her from Randolph."

"But now Mac's in that bed fighting for his life because of that idea."

"Can you convince her to go back?" Ray asked hopefully. "Right now. Tonight."

"You don't know Sage very well, do you?" Ben grinned. "No one convinces her to do something she doesn't want to do."

"Look," Ray began, then stepped up closer to Ben. "I'm working on an angle right now . . ."

"What kind of angle?"

"I'm sorry. I'm not at liberty."

"You want my help and yet you won't level with me?" Ben asked incredulously, then he looked Ray square in the eye. "What kind of angle?"

"To tell you the truth," he said reluctantly, "I thought if Ms. McColl believed she was a suspect in her father's attack, it might keep her in hiding."

"So you had no intention of drawing her out."

"We've linked Randolph to someone very close to Ms. McColl," Ray replied. "I want to follow up on it, but I can't be looking over my shoulder all the time to make sure she is tucked away safely somewhere. If you care about this woman at all, you'll drag her kicking and screaming across that border if you have to, and you'll hog-tie her until we get Randolph into custody."

"Across the border," Ben repeated. "You knew where she was?"

"Of course I knew," he shrugged. "I'm a cop. I made it my business to know."

"And you want me to just toss her over my shoulder and take her back with me," Ben repeated, just for clarity.

Ben jerked his head upright and looked into Sage's eyes where she was suddenly standing in the doorway.

"I'm not going anywhere, Detective Martin," she said, then dragged her gaze away from Ben and across the corridor to Ray. "Kicking and screaming, or any other way. My father needs to know I'm here."

"Your father needs to know you're safe," Ray corrected. "And we couldn't guarantee him that with you out in the open like this."

"Detective . . ."

"Look, young lady," Ray urged, "do you have any idea what you're dealing with here? Eric Randolph has made no bones about the fact that he is hunting you down. When he finds you, he's going to make sure you are never available to testify about anything having to do with him. He's not messing around here."

"No, the holes in my father's chest and head were my first clues, Detective."

Ray heaved a deep, meaningful sigh.

"Raymond."

"What?"

"My name is Raymond," he told her softly. "Call me Ray."

Ben could see that Sage didn't know what to say to that.

"I'm sorry about your father, Ms. McColl," Ray softly continued. "God knows, I couldn't be more sorry. But you're at issue just as well as he is. He wanted you somewhere safe." He shrugged, adding, "And this ain't it."

"Detective," Ben interjected, then stopped himself. "Ray."

He nodded, and they exchange half-smiles.

"Sage has been through an awful lot. Let me take her back to our motel to get some sleep. In the morning, we'll talk about it, and she'll call you tomorrow."

"How can I let her just walk out there on her own?" Ray asked sincerely. "If Randolph finds out . . ."

"He won't," Ben promised confidently. "We'll call you tomorrow."

Ben slipped his arm over Sage's shoulders and led her down the hall. He was bone-tired in a way he hadn't been since Laura's illness. There was something about hospitals . . .

A uniformed officer turned the corner and headed straight for them. Even though he trusted Ray to let them leave, Ben's heart pounded just a little harder until the officer had passed.

"Here to relieve you, sir," he greeted Ray as Ben pushed the button for the elevator. "You ready to get some sleep?"

"Not yet, Bates," Ray replied. "I just want to look in on McColl one more time."

The hum of the heater was the only thing that broke the silence as they drove along toward the motel. It was a chilly night, even for autumn in Southern California.

"Are you warm enough?" Ben asked, and Sage tiredly nodded, never taking her eyes off the reflection of lights on the windshield.

"How about food? Are you hungry?"

"No," she managed. And then, "Yes."

"Well, that's progress," he said aloud, then grinned. "What would you like? Something you can't get in Mexico."

"A Tony burger," she considered. "And a large vanilla shake. They're open all night."

"And do tell, what is a Tony burger?" he asked.

"Really bad burger," she replied. "Smothered in the greasiest chili you've ever eaten."

"Sounds wonderful," he said, making a face to express his sarcasm.

"You'll see. It's the best."

Ben was astounded at how much effect this small creature's frame of mind had on his own. A hint of relief shining from her tattered emotions caused his own to soar without measure.

"A Tony burger it is then," he nodded, rubbing her arm gently as he drove on. "Just tell me how to get there."

"Make a left at the next street," she said, pointing. "So, what do you think, Ben?"

"I love burgers. I'm good with it."

"No," she chuckled, and he looked at her curiously. "About me going back to Mexico."

"I can't make that decision for you," he said cautiously.

"I don't want you to make it for me. I want your counsel."

"Well, in that case," he replied. "I suppose I'd counsel you to do what Ray wants you to do. Go back into hiding and stay there. Let law enforcement do their jobs."

"How?" she asked emotionally. "That's it, right up there on the left. You saw him lying there. How can I just leave him?"

"I know how much that hurt you," he said as he rounded the corner into the parking lot. "If you want to stay here, Sage, I'll stay with you. Whatever you decide."

"You can't stay here, Ben. What about the problems at the orphanage?"

"I'm needed there," he admitted. "But I'm needed

here, too. If something happened to you, I don't know what I'd—"

He cut himself off abruptly.

"You have to go back," she confirmed, dancing adeptly around his indication of feelings she suspected but had never looked at, head-on. "You can't stay here because of me."

"I'm not going back without you, Sage."

Ben slowed the pickup to a stop in between the faded white lines in the parking lot, and he and Sage stared into each other's eyes for several long moments.

"I'm not going back without you," he repeated. "I can't just leave you here."

"Then you know how I feel about leaving my father," she pointed out, and Ben nodded.

"Tony burger and a vanilla shake," he repeated. "You stay in the car."

"Eric's not going to be out here at this time of night," she insisted. "I'll go with you."

Ben took a quick look at the dashboard clock. 3:10 A.M. There were half a dozen people milling around the walk-up counter of Tony's, every one of them someone he would suspect of crimes untold.

"Humor me," he said firmly. "Stay in the car."

"But . . ."

"Sage."

"Oh, all right," she agreed at last. "But get one for Beth. She's got to be as ripe for some good old American junk food as I am!"

When they had returned to the hotel, Sage's room was completely dark, and she could hear Beth's deep, restful breathing when she poked her head in the door.

"She's sleeping," Sage whispered, pulling the door shut for a moment. "Do you want to split hers?"

"You didn't get enough with your own?" Ben asked incredulously. "Now you want another one?"

Sage slurped at her milkshake and nodded. "Mmmm-hmmm."

"All right, lock the door." He grinned. "Come to my room."

Sage obeyed, and followed Ben next door. Once inside, he turned and handed her the cardboard box bearing one more greasy, wonderful Tony burger.

"These things are lethal," he said, pushing a fist to the center of his chest and forcing a puff of air out comedically.

"I've had a lot of Tony burgers in my day, Ben Travis," Sage said, plopping down on one of the two beds and going at the wax wrap around the sandwich.

"I'll just bet you have," he replied, and Sage noticed a sort of sleepy sadness in his eyes.

"Want to split?" she offered.

"No!" he exclaimed. "You go right ahead."

Ben sat down on the opposite bed and watched her carefully, then shook his head and smiled.

"What?" she asked self-consciously.

"Don't get me wrong," he began, then turned serious. "I'm happy to see your improved frame of mind."

"Food does that to me," she told him.

"I believe you're using that term loosely when it comes to these burgers," he observed. "But you're not going to get any sleep tonight, Sage. You can't eat like that at three in the morning and expect to get any rest."

"Oh no?" She rose to his challenge. "You just watch me."

Sage knew Ben could never understand that part of her life that allowed her to eat Tony burgers at 3 A.M., or roast beef sandwiches at dawn like the one she'd made when she'd met him in her father's darkened kitchen so long ago.

She remembered thinking he was adorable. But the truth was that someone like Ben Travis could never have fit into her lifestyle. Partying until dawn, and then sleeping into the afternoon, eating whatever struck her, whenever it struck her; virtually no stress beyond choosing between shopping and a day at Elizabeth Arden. A career and an adult life had been brushed aside for the comfort and safety of her family home (and family money), and these were choices a man like Ben Travis couldn't possibly abide.

She remembered that she'd made a conscious plan to enable her to continue life as she knew it. She'd thought that if she was lucky enough to entice Eric into proposing, she might never have to make the transition from total freedom to a life of grown-up concerns about money management, career, and whatever else the rest of the women in the world had to worry about. Oh, how life had changed for her. Just a few weeks ago seemed like an eternity to her now.

"All right then," Ben shrugged, nodding toward the burger. "Knock yourself out."

Sage looked down at the uneaten delicacy, and something inside her curled up a little. Maybe he was right, although she'd rather digest nails than admit that to him.

"I want to get Beth to a doctor first thing tomorrow,"

Ben told her, as he unfastened the laces of his work boots. "Something's not right about this back pain, and I aim to find out what it is."

"That's a good idea," Sage nodded, suppressing a yawn behind her hand. "She has a doctor here in town, I think."

"I'll talk to her in the morning."

"I wonder how Miguel's cold is doing," Sage found herself thinking aloud, her eyes closed.

"He has a cold?"

"Oh, well, sniffles really," she replied casually, stretching out sideways on the bed as she brushed aside the cardboard-boxed sandwich. She allowed herself an unceremonious yawn before continuing. "I hope Maria remembers to use those nose drops in the medical kit."

Her body had begun to relax, and Sage was halfway to the edge of sleep before she even realized it.

"Hey." Ben's voice called her back from the threshold. "What happened to that chili burger you wanted so much?"

"Mmmmm," she sighed. "No thank you."

And then there it was again. The blessed, peaceful blackness of sleep that she needed to reach out for more than she could even comprehend.

"Sage? Come on, sweetheart," she heard Ben say softly as his arms gathered her upright.

"No, no," she pleaded. "Leave me alone. I just need to sleep."

"You can sleep next door," he assured her, and he lifted her from the bed.

Sage vaguely comprehended what was happening as the cool air of the San Diego night assaulted her, and then there was the warmth again that she craved. Warm blankets made their way over her, and a soft, fragrant pillow nestled her head as she drifted down, down, down once more to that lovely place she so desperately craved.

Ben lay awake for a long time after that, his arms folded behind his head, staring at the darkness between himself and the ceiling.

So many things to work out, he thought. *So many questions.*

His eyes burned from exhaustion, and yet he fought the sleep that would have happily engulfed him had he given in to it. Mac's lifeless body floated across his mind, and he felt Sage's pain afresh.

Perhaps it takes a tragedy like this to make a person stop and think.

The comment seemed to be his own thought, and yet foreign, as if spoken in another tongue. A twinge of guilt pierced his chest. Sage wasn't a bad person in need of something horrible to catapult her into reality; she was innately wonderful, really. She had just made some poor choices. And being raised in an atmosphere of such privilege could only have resulted in what she had become. Not that she was such a bad person, even in the beginning. A little spoiled, yes. But not bad. Not Sage.

She had changed so much, Ben admitted to himself. Seeing her with the children, with baby Miguel, he had noticed a spark of goodness ignite inside her. She had even prayed with them on occasion.

What am I thinking? he suddenly asked himself. *Am I actually gauging her progress toward being someone I could commit to?*

Ben didn't like the thought, and he tried to sweep it away by rolling over to his side and burrowing his head into the pillow.

The two of them could never be a couple; they were too vastly different. And then the word crept back upon him.

Couple.

"Are you out of your mind?" he exclaimed aloud, then tossed over to his other side and hunkered down into the blankets.

Just about the time that he let go and allowed himself to drift away on the wings of sleep, a picture of Sage passed over his consciousness. She was lying there in her bed, the sweetest smile on her fresh-scrubbed face. He had tucked the blankets under her chin, and brushed her hair away to get a full view of that smile that contained so much peace. Love. Trust.

Ben tossed himself over one more time to his opposite side, punched at the pillow twice, then dropped his head onto it.

A couple indeed. Sage McColl would never couple with the likes of me anyway.

Chapter Eleven

Sage's eyes fluttered fully open, then fell back into a squint at the light of day streaming through the opening between two heavy drapes. She shielded her eyes with one hand, and pushed herself upright with the other. Beth wasn't in the other bed, and she could see by the mirror that the bathroom door was open, the room dark and unoccupied.

She climbed from the bed and stretched every muscle in her stiff body before flipping on the light that hung over a table and chairs near the window. There, on paper bearing the motel logo, was what looked to be a hastily scribbled note.

Taken Beth to the doctor. Stay put.
                                    Ben

"Yes, sir," she saluted, then tossed the note to the side and picked up the phone. "Do you have room service?" she asked when the attendant answered the phone.

"No, ma'am," came the answer, and it sounded almost as if the woman on the other end of the line wanted to laugh right out loud.

"Oh. Well, what time is it?"

"It is now 1:43 in the afternoon," the woman stated impatiently.

No wonder she was so hungry. Sage paused to give thought to the question of finding something to eat, and she heard the woman tapping something, probably a pencil tip on the base of her phone.

"Where can I get something to eat around here?" she asked.

"There's a Denny's on the corner," the woman provided in monotone. "Or a McDonald's up the next block."

Sage wasn't sure which prospect was bleaker. "All right, thank you," she said, and abruptly put down the phone before the woman could slam down the receiver.

One more stretch, and she wandered into the bathroom. She ran steamy water into the tub and rummaged through the basket on the counter for something for the bath.

Conditioner. Body Lotion.

The only thing with bubbles was shampoo, so she decided to forego the amenities and indulge in a simple hot bath. Sage lowered herself into the water slowly, then eased back against the porcelain tub. It was heaven. Sheer heaven. Had she only been in Mexico a few weeks? It seemed like an eternity. And now, even the primitive surroundings of the inferior motel chain were like a slice of personal paradise.

She made a silent wish that she could melt the two worlds together. Ben and Beth, the children and Miguel . . . combined with civilization and espresso and hot bubble baths. Was there really something so wrong in that wish? she wondered.

Why can't it happen?

Thoughts of this side of her parallel universe slid sleekly over her just as the warm water cascaded down her body from a scrunched-up washcloth. She longed to take a cool dip in the pool and tread water beneath the cascading waterfall at home; have lemonade on the veranda with her father overlooking her mother's precious rose garden; poke around the antique stores in the Gaslamp District with Connie.

The thought of Connie stirred a brew of anticipation inside her, and Sage immediately rose from the tub and wrapped herself in the thin terrycloth towel from the metal rack.

Leaving the water standing in the tub, she hurried straight to the telephone and dialed. Just to hear the voice of her friend again! She was so excited that butterflies rose in her stomach.

"Connie?" She beamed. "Is that you?"

"Sage?"

Her friend sounded startled. Almost frightened.

"Where are you, sweetie?"

"Long story," Sage breathed.

"You know about Mac?"

"Yes, I've seen him," Sage admitted. "It's horrible."

"You've seen him? So you're here in town then?"

"I couldn't stay away." She sighed. "Not once I'd heard what Eric had done."

"Do you know for certain that it was Eric? You know they're saying it might have been you."

"That's a long story, too," Sage told her. "But I'm not in any danger of being charged. Surely you knew it couldn't be true."

"Of course I did. Sweetie, you're my best friend. Who knows you better than I do?"

"Oh, Connie, I'm so tired. And so homesick, and afraid. And I miss you so much I could just about die."

"Tell me where you are. I'll come and get you," her friend offered excitedly. "We'll go to Gleason's for a trout salad."

"Mmmmm, that sounds like heaven," she said, and closed her eyes to remember the elegance and ambiance of one of her favorite lunch spots with her girlfriends.

"I don't know," she said then. "I don't think I should just be wandering out and about like that."

"Why not? You're not the one who's guilty! It's Eric who should be sneaking around, deprived of his normal life."

"That will happen soon enough, I'm sure," Sage assured her.

"So where are you? I'll be very careful, and I won't tell a soul where I'm going. I want to see you and make sure for myself that you're all right."

"I'm really fine." Sage shrugged. "Tired. Hungry for a trout salad."

They shared a giggle over that, and Sage sighed.

"Oh, I don't know. Ben would just flip if . . ."

She stopped herself, but the reference wasn't lost on Connie.

"Ben? Who's Ben?"

A million responses turned over inside of her, but none of them would come out.

"A guy I met while I was hiding out," she chose.

"I've got to hear the details!" Connie pleaded. "Come on, you can't leave me in the dark."

"Oh, all right," Sage laughed excitedly. "I'll tell you over lunch."

"Great! Where are you?"

"Just beyond Old Town," she revealed. "At the corner across from that little Mexican place with the tacky veranda."

"By the Denny's?" Connie groaned. "Why?"

Sage chuckled out loud, then said, "I'll meet you on the corner in thirty minutes."

"Sweetie, I can't wait to see you."

"Me either, Connie. I need my best friend."

Ben rose from the leather chair for the umpteenth time and began to pace to and fro across the small waiting area. Beth had been in with her doctor for what seemed like hours, and his heart raced a little faster with every few minutes that passed. He recalled a similar situation in a doctor's office, and he felt the thud of his heart as it fell within him.

This can't be the same as Laura. It can't be.

Like Laura, Beth was a good woman. A woman devoted to serving God by loving others. A woman with a pure heart and a driving desire to meet the many needs of the less fortunate.

Don't let her die, he found himself thinking as he plunked back down into the chair.

When the door opened and Beth stepped through, a smile decorating her face, Ben felt as if he were breathing for the first time in an hour.

"Ben Travis, I swear," she declared, "you look as if you haven't slept in a month."

"Have I?" he joked without smiling. "I can't remember."

Beth signed something at the desk, and then lolled her canvas bag over her shoulder with a wince.

"What is it?" Ben asked helplessly, raising his hands as if preparing to catch her if she fell. "What did he say?"

"I told you what it was," she teased him with a little pinch to his arm. "It's my sciatica. Same as always."

Ben looked at her as if he didn't believe a word she was saying, and he guessed that, deep down, maybe he didn't.

"It's the nerve that runs from . . ."

"I know what it is," he interrupted. "He's sure that's all it is? You just looked to be in so much pain."

"Well, honey, it's painful." She grinned, then gasped as the realization hit her. "Oooh, Ben."

"What?"

She took him by the arm and led him to an unoccupied corner of the waiting room, pointing to a chair as she carefully lowered herself to the one beside it. Ben obediently sat down.

"Ben. Have you been thinking of Laura all this time?"

How could he respond to that? Not a day passed that he didn't think of his wife.

"What do you mean?"

"I mean this back pain," she said knowingly. "You've convinced yourself that it's Laura all over again, haven't you?"

Ben looked down at his shoes. Why, when she said it out loud, did it sound so foolish?

"Ben."

When he didn't look up, Beth cupped his chin in her hand and raised his face.

"It's my back, Ben. I promise you. It's nothing more than a pinched sciatica nerve. It's very painful, but it's treatable. I'll be fine in a matter of a week or so."

He was mortified when a small well of tears rose in his eyes and streamed out without warning, and he wiped them away quickly with the back of his hand.

"You loved her so deeply," she said softly, then put her arms around him and kissed his cheek tenderly. "I should have seen why you were so concerned about my ailment. I didn't realize. I'm sorry, honey."

"Sorry?" he asked, willing away the last trace of his weakness. "You didn't do anything to be sorry for."

"Yes, I'm afraid I did." She beamed. "I wasn't clear enough with you about what was going on. And I brought Sage into your life without warning."

"You needn't warn me about Sage," he said as he shook his head.

"Oh, yes, I do need to. I've known from the first time I saw the two of you together at Mac's home that there were storms brewing. I didn't plan it, but when Sage needed refuge it seemed to me to be ordained."

"Beth, you are out of your tree, do you know that?"

"I should have realized that falling in love with Sage was going to bring up all those unresolved feelings in you about losing Laura," she said, and he felt somewhat angry at her assumption.

"Falling in love with Sage," he repeated, and his eyebrows came together in a serious glare. "Don't be absurd."

She tapped on the center of his chest with her index finger and smiled sweetly. "You know in here that it's not absurd at all. Don't you, Ben?"

"We couldn't be more different," he objected. "She could never . . ."

"Oh, I think she could, Ben," Beth interjected. "As a matter of fact, I think she does."

Ben's heart began to pound, and the truth of her statement engulfed him in its intensity. He did love Sage. He loved her! He had no doubt about it.

"I want you to promise me something," Beth said softly.

"Name it," he replied without looking up.

"You'll take Sage back to Mexico with you today," she said.

"She won't go with me," he retorted. "Not with Mac in that hospital all alone."

"He won't be all alone," she said confidently.

"What do you mean?"

"He won't be alone," she explained, "because I'll be with him."

"You'll . . . ? What? What did the doctor really say?"

"No, no," she said, gently massaging his shoulder in an effort to keep him seated. "I'm not being admitted. I want to stay here with Mac."

"What?" Ben asked, scratching the side of his jaw as he turned the idea around in his head. "Why?"

"Because, you know how you feel about Sage?" she asked him, and Ben reluctantly nodded. "Well, that's how I feel about her father."

Chapter Twelve

Sage paced restlessly on the corner as she waited for Connie. The girl was born late and had never recovered; she didn't know why she hadn't remembered that until now.

She looked around at the passers-by, at the couple of tough-looking men in the Denny's parking lot, at the convertible junker that slowed to take an extended look at her as it rounded the corner. She regretted the decision to meet up with Connie and, just about the time she was considering heading back over to the hotel to call off the meeting, Connie's BMW made a U-turn in the middle of traffic and stopped in front of her.

"You look horrible" were the first words out of Connie's mouth as she leaned over to push open the passenger side door. "Hurry and get in before you get mugged."

Sage slid into the car and hugged her friend enthusiastically, then Connie took a lock of Sage's hair into her hands and grimaced.

"Or have you already been mugged?"

"Oh, hush." Sage snickered. "Let's go."

Connie peeled her car around the corner, and Sage realized another thing she'd forgotten about her friend: she drove like one of the Andretti family.

"At least put some makeup on," Connie said, shoving her bag toward Sage. "You look like death."

"You don't love me unless I look perfect?"

"Well, I don't want to sit in Gleason's across from you looking like *that*." She pouted. "I won't be able to digest my meal."

"Thank you so much," she replied sarcastically.

"Now tell me everything," Connie said, reaching into the pocket of the bag and producing a liquid concealer stick. "Start with those circles under your eyes, sweetie. You look undernourished."

Sage unfolded the lighted visor and looked at herself in the reflection. Connie was right! She did look a fright.

"Who . . . is . . . Ben?" she asked dramatically, and Sage smiled.

"I told you. Just a guy I met."

"Where did you meet him?" she pushed. "And while we're at it, where have you been?"

"Do we have to talk about that just yet?" Sage grimaced. "Can't you fill me in on the local gossip? And what happened with that guy from Firestorm you were going to go out with?"

At the same time they both crooned, "Jimm-mmy," then cackled with laughter.

While Connie chatted on about the delectable Jimmy and the local crew of friends and acquaintances, offering a fair amount of San Diego scandal, Sage wondered why she was so reluctant to tell her friend about Ben. And more specifically about the intensity of her feelings for him.

She attributed it to her friend's, well, shallowness. Connie would never allow herself to fall for any man who wasn't listed somewhere within the text of the local social register, and certainly not someone who devoted his life to a cause which kept him holed up in the pocket of nothing less than poverty.

But Ben is rich in other ways, she found herself thinking, then gasped as Connie poked her in the side with a jab of her elbow.

"Are you even listening to me?" she cried.

"I'm sorry," Sage said. "I was just thinking."

"About what?" her friend asked curiously.

After a long pause, Sage grinned. "About Gleason's trout salad! I'm starved."

"Then you're forgiven," her friend stated with a nod.

Ben had begun working out in his mind what he would say to Sage on the drive back from the doctor's office, and he had decided on a final draft while standing in line at the pharmacy filling Beth's prescription. He would let Beth reveal her secret to Sage, and tell her that she intended to stay at Mac's side for as long as he needed her. And then he would join in, making his case for taking her back to Mexico with him until Ray could implement his plan to bring Randolph into custody.

And after that? he asked himself, then shook the

thought away. *I have no right to think about the future with Sage. Just stick to the present and handle the crises at hand.*

"I'll bet our girl is starving by now," Beth said, as she rapped on the door, then unlocked it with her key.

"I'll be surprised if our girl is even awake," Ben added cheerfully.

"Sage?" Beth called out when they entered the dark, empty room. "Honey?"

She wandered past the beds and poked her head around the corner into the bathroom. Water stood in the tub and was as smooth as glass.

"Where could she be?" she asked Ben, and he looked around, perplexed. "Maybe she was hungry."

Ben's gaze settled on a small piece of paper standing at the center of the table, resting against a plastic ashtray. Picking it up, he flicked on the overhead light.

"Be back soon," he read aloud, drawing Beth's full attention. "Having trout salad at Gleason's with Connie."

"Connie!" Beth exclaimed. "Has that girl lost her mind? She wasn't supposed to tell a soul where she was."

"Gleason's. Where is it?"

"Down at the waterfront," Beth said, and, before she could give him further details, Ben raced out of the room.

Forcing himself to breathe rhythmically, Ben ignored the pounding in his chest and the backbeat of worry that churned inside him. He was suddenly reminded of Ray's words about there being someone close to Sage who was in communication with Randolph.

If only I'd have told her what Ray said. There were

just so many other things going on . . . I should have made sure she understood . . .

"Oh, I've missed this town so much!" Sage exclaimed, stopping to paw through a street cart outside a rare bookstore.

"Now that's it. Tell me where you've been," Connie insisted, as she tried on a vintage shawl from a rack outside the consignment store next door.

"Look at this," Sage said curiously, then opened the leather-bound book and peered inside. *"Love Letters for the Ages,"* she said, reading the title aloud. "It's letters exchanged between famous couples."

Napoleon and Josephine; Lord Randolph Churchill and Jennie Jerome; Mozart and his wife.

What a delightful book! she thought just as the clerk appeared in the doorway.

"May I help you, ma'am?"

"How much is this?" she asked him.

"The price is inside the cover," he replied, moving toward her to check the flap. "Fifteen dollars."

"Yes, I'll take it," she told him, digging a credit card out of her purse and handing it over.

While Connie used the ladies' room and Sage waited to be led through Gleason's to a table near the window, she flipped casually through the book, stopping at a page bearing the name of her favorite poet, Elizabeth Barrett Browning.

It seems to me, to myself, that no man was ever before to any woman what you are to me, she read, and a flock of butterflies rose and fell inside her. Never had the words of a poet rung so true in her heart. She pushed away the feeling and shut the book tight as Connie reappeared just in time to join her.

"A bottle of chardonnay," Connie instructed the waiter before she was even seated.

"None for me," Sage corrected. "I'd like a Perrier."

"Oh. Well." Connie eyed her curiously, then amended, "Just a glass for me then. And perhaps an order of those darling little salmon appetizers you make. I just love those."

"Yes, ma'am." The waiter nodded, then headed off hurriedly to fulfill their requests.

"Oh!" Sage sighed. "I've missed this."

"I've missed you," her friend stated. "Why didn't you call me and let me know you were all right?"

"I couldn't," she said apologetically. "Daddy was very clear that he wanted me talking with absolutely no one until Eric was found."

"And now . . ." Connie began, then shook her head. "Poor Mac."

"I'm so frightened for him, Connie. He looks so frail and alone."

"He'll be all right, sweetie. He just has to be."

Ben didn't know at first how Ray knew to be at Gleason's, but their cars squealed up in front of the restaurant at just about the same instant, from perfectly opposite directions. Beth crossed his mind suddenly and he realized she had placed the call.

"Is she here?" Ray asked, running toward the front door.

"I don't know," Ben told him, and jogged after him into the restaurant. "Is she the one? Is it Connie?"

Ray scanned the entire place, then turned seriously toward Ben and nodded. "It's her."

"No!" Ben cried out, then pounded his fist hard against the stucco wall as Ray flashed his badge to the waiter and asked him several questions.

"Thanks," Ray said, then tugged on Ben's sleeve as he hurried out the door.

Peering up the street and then down, Ray stood poised and ready.

"There!" Ben shouted, pointing to the BMW parked up the block. Sage was just about to lower herself into the passenger seat.

"Sage!" he cried out, but she didn't seem to hear. "Sage!"

She looked back at him, and her entire face seemed to be set ablaze with her smile.

"Ben!" she called back to him with a grin as wide as he'd ever seen. His entire body relaxed with relief.

Suddenly, out of nowhere, masculine arms stretched out from the back seat of the BMW and pulled her into the car. Sage was screaming as Ray and Ben bounded up the sidewalk toward her.

"No, no," she cried, but they were too late. The car pulled away from the curb, Connie at the wheel and Graham in the backseat holding Sage to the seat by the throat.

Just a few more yards and I could have helped her. Ben's heart lurched inside him as he looked down at his feet. Her purse lay open, its contents scattered about the leather-bound book that was all she'd left behind. He picked up the book and read the title, then clutched it to his chest.

The gunshots that rang out were followed by the ear-splitting squeal of tires. Startled, Ben reeled around to find that Ray had gone off in pursuit of the car on foot. When that attempt failed, he had drawn his weapon and expertly fired. Connie's vehicle screeched out of control as her tire went flat, and the crash was deafening as they landed against a storefront on the far side of the street.

The adrenaline rush coursing through Ben's entire body catapulted him into action, and he felt as if he were running so quickly that he might stumble over his own feet.

Ray turned to one of the passers-by and shouted, "Call 911 for back-up," then held his gun firm as he crossed the street and approached the car.

"Ben, get back!" he warned, hardly taking his eye off the crumpled car for even a moment, but Ben had no intention of stepping back.

The patrons of the Italian restaurant that had been invaded by the crash milled about on the other side of the broken plate-glass window, in a daze, awestruck.

"Is everyone all right?" Ray called, his gun still leveled at Connie's car. "Is anyone hurt?"

"I don't think so," someone yelled back.

"Get away from the car," he instructed them. "Ben, tell them to clear the way."

Ben rounded the crash and motioned people away as he scanned the wreckage for any sign of life.

She has to be alive. Dear God, let her be alive.

He found himself still clutching her purse and the leather book as he looked to Ray for further instruction. Suddenly, there was movement inside the car, and Ben groaned out in relief as a mane of fire-red curls appeared inside the window. She tried several times to open the door, but it was jammed shut, so she pulled herself up and over and began, head first, to climb out the window.

"Sage," Ben laughed. "Thank God! Sage."

Ignoring Raymond's second warning to step back, Ben jogged toward her and, tossing her purse and the book to the ground, he took her into his arms and lifted her out of the wreck. As he planted kisses on her head, face and shoulders, her blood smeared his face with slippery splotches of red. He cradled her in his arms and walked away from the car, content to let Ray handle whatever came next. She was all he cared about, all he needed to concern himself with.

When he set her feet on the ground and began to let go, she swooned and nearly fell. Ben picked her up into his arms again and moved further down the sidewalk to a wrought-iron bench outside a small coffeehouse.

"Ben?" she moaned, and he saw that her face was sparkling with countless shards of broken glass.

"I'm here," he told her as he began gently picking them off her eyelids. "I'm here."

"I love you," she whispered hoarsely, and Ben froze for a long moment.

"I love you, too," he replied, but she hadn't heard him before slipping out of consciousness.

Chapter Thirteen

"When will this nightmare ever end?" Sage wept, and she took great solace in Ben's arms as he leaned across the hospital bed to hold her.

"Soon," he promised, and something about his tone of voice made it almost possible for her to believe him. "Now that Graham is gone, he'll have to come out in the open to do his dirty work. And Ray's going to catch him. You'll see."

"They said Graham died instantly in the crash," Sage observed as Ben looked Ray in the eye.

"I can't believe . . . Connie," Sage said for the dozenth time. "I just can't believe it."

"She's fessed up to everything," Ray assured her, and the truth cut through her like a double-edged knife.

She was my best friend.

She held the words deep within her heart, and mourned the deception inside of them.

She betrayed me.

"The plan was to maneuver you to Vegas to marry Randolph," Ray filled them in. "A wife cannot be forced to testify against her husband, and so . . . no witness, no evidence, no charges."

"I would never have married him now!" she exclaimed adamantly.

"I don't think he planned to give you much choice in the matter," Ben added.

"Did you ever tell Connie where you'd been hiding all this time?" Ray asked curiously.

"No," she replied with the shake of her head. "I just had a feeling about that."

"Good instincts," Ray commended her. "Now I need you to follow *my* good instincts."

"Go back to Mexico?" she asked him knowingly, and Raymond nodded his head.

"Please, Ms. McColl. Surely you can see it's too dangerous for you to . . ."

"Sage," she said softly. "You can call me Sage."

Ray gave her a grin that reminded her how good-looking he really was, then patted her lightly on the arm before extending a handshake toward Ben.

"Good work today," Ben told him. "You're a good cop."

"Now she's in your hands, Travis," Ray said. "Get her out of here without delay."

Ben nodded, and they watched Ray take his leave.

"I can't leave my father all alone, Ben," Sage whimpered the moment they were alone. "I just can't."

"Sweetheart," he began, then paused to stroke her hair

and the side of her face. "Did you know that Beth is in love with your father?"

"What? What's that got to do with . . ."

"Well," he tried again, but she interrupted him with the wave of her hand.

"Beth and Daddy have always been close," she reasoned. "She was my mother's dearest friend."

Ben smiled at her. "There's a little more to it, Sage. And because of that, Beth has decided to stay here with Mac. She doesn't want him to be alone either and . . ."

"Wait a minute!" she interrupted, shaking the fog from her head. "What are you saying?"

"I'm saying . . ."

"Beth is in love with my father?" she finished for him. "Where did you get a crazy idea like that?"

"From Beth," he stated matter-of-factly. "Does it bother you?"

"Bother me," she repeated thoughtfully.

"I'm eager to hear the answer to that question myself."

They looked up to find Beth standing in the doorway. Her sheepish grin transformed itself almost immediately to a confident arched brow over a questioning smile.

"Does the idea bother you?" she asked Sage carefully, then limped into the room and sat on the bed beside her.

"Of course not," Sage told her. "I mean, no. But . . . well . . . does Daddy know?"

"Yes," she chuckled. "He knows."

"He never mentioned a word."

"I'm going to stay here with him, honey," Beth said as she took Sage by the hand. "And I promise to keep you aware of everything as it happens. But, from what I understand from the officer who brought me over here, you cannot afford to take any more chances with your safety. You need to go back with Ben."

"But I can't just leave him," she protested, and Beth gave her hand a squeeze.

"It's what he would tell you to do," she told Sage. "And you know that's the truth."

Sage felt ten years old again, and she imagined she looked like a pathetic doe caught in the headlights of a speeding car. Although it wasn't a conscious choice, her gaze darted to Ben for his input. He nodded, and she was delivered. All indecision melted away with one look from Ben, and the weight of that fact was not in the least bit lost on anyone present.

"All right," she finally said. "But you'll call me every day."

"Yes."

"Whether there's something to tell or not." She wagged her finger.

"Yes."

"And even if you don't think he can hear you," she said as she battled the tears back from her eyes, "you'll tell him every day that I love him."

Beth took Sage into her arms and chuckled, deep and throaty. "Oh, he knows that, honey," she soothed. "But I'll remind him every day."

It was a small assurance, but Sage took hold of it as the lifeline that it was. She knew if Mac were awake and calling the shots again, he would demand that she return to Mexico, and no amount of whining or objections would change his mind once he'd issued his high command.

"We'll leave right away," Ben announced, and she

could sense the relief in his eyes. "As soon as they can process your release."

"I don't feel right leaving you," Sage whispered, her father's lifeless hand clasped between her own. "But Beth is right. If you could tell me what to do this instant, you would tell me to go back with Ben."

She cautiously shot a glance in each direction, then leaned in close to his ear.

"Daddy, I think I'm in love with Ben Travis," she whispered, bemused. "Can you imagine anything more ridiculous?"

For only an instant, she thought he'd gripped her hand tighter, then dismissed it for what it was: wishful thinking.

"And I can't believe you didn't tell me about you and Beth," she said, wiping tears from her cheeks with the back of her hand. "Did you think I wouldn't approve? Well, I approve, Daddy. Beth is a wonderful woman. She's already part of the family anyway. But you've really got to learn to open up to me more. I should have heard that from you, not from Ben and Beth. Can you hear me, Daddy? I'm being very serious here. I want us to be closer when you wake up. I want you to be . . ."

Sage paused for a long moment, drinking in her father's suntanned face, tracing the laugh lines near his eyes with her finger.

"I want you to be proud of me," she whispered. "I promise I'll make you proud, Daddy. Just please . . . come back to me."

*   *   *

Ben had allotted ten minutes for Sage to run into the house and gather a few more of her things to take along with her across the border. As they pulled into the drive and the truck came to a stop, she threw open the door.

"Synchronize our watches," she exclaimed, and Ben reveled in her teasing manner with him.

"Ten minutes, McColl," he warned, and she saluted flippantly.

"I'll be ready in nine." She grinned, then burst through the front door and ran up the curved staircase.

Ben followed at a much slower pace, passing through the gaping doorway and closing the door behind him.

"May I help you?" Cook asked sternly as he walked confidently into the foyer.

"I'm with Ms. McColl," he stated. "She's upstairs."

"Miss Sage," Cook clarified, and Ben nodded. "And she is safe?"

Ben nodded.

"She is aware then of her father's condition?"

"Yes. She's been at the hospital with him today," Ben explained.

"And?"

"No," Ben told him sadly. "No change."

Cook's shoulders dropped in disappointment, and Ben felt for the man. He was on the outside of a situation which so obviously affected the inside of this man's life; apart from Mac being his sole means of support, the affection he possessed for his employer was clear.

The fragrance of something chocolate baking in the kitchen teased Ben's senses. It apparently did the same to Sage as she floated down the stairway, seemingly led by her nose.

"Are those brownies I smell?" she asked the older man, whose stoic demeanor did not change.

"Your father's favorite, Miss," he nodded. "To enjoy when he returns home."

Ben could see that the moment was not lost on Sage as her entire beautiful face softened and she brushed her hand over Cook's shoulder.

"That's a lovely thought," she told him hoarsely. "Daddy would love it that you're preparing for his homecoming."

"Thank you, Miss," he replied.

Sage stared hard at the man for a long moment, and Cook fidgeted uneasily beneath her gaze.

"Will you be needing your quarters prepared?" he asked, casting a brief glance at the duffel bag she had dropped at the foot of the stairs.

"No." Sage smiled gratefully, then as sudden and soft as a whisper, she pulled the man into a brief hug. "You're so important to our family, Harry. Thank you so much for all that you do."

"Y-yes," he stammered. "Th-thank you, Miss."

He was obviously unaccustomed to being startled out of his professional formality, and Ben suppressed a smile by turning away casually.

"Serving your family has always been my pleasure."

"Mr. Travis and I will be going," she said with a lopsided grin and a quick look at Ben that told him she was amused by Cook's sudden discomfort. "Would you mind packing us a little something for the road?"

"Certainly, Miss," he said.

"Also, Beth Wayans will be arriving sometime this evening," she instructed. "She'll be staying here while

Daddy is in the hospital. Please tell the staff they are to behave with her as if she were the lady of the house."

"Yes, Miss," he nodded, and Sage curiously regarded the expression on the man's face as he retreated toward the kitchen.

"I'll bet he's thinking how horrible I am to leave while Daddy's lying in that hospital bed," Sage said as she moved nearer to Ben. "And he's right."

"No, he's not right," Ben soothed, easing her into his embrace.

When she released her gentle hold on him, Ben was instantly reminded of the feeling of a bandage being yanked away from his sensitive adolescent shin.

"I-Is that your bag?"

Well, of course it's her bag, you idiot. That's all you can think of to say after just a simple hug? It was nothing more, for crying out loud. Just a hug.

He wondered if she'd felt the heat of it, too.

Sage looked at the bottom of the stairs where Ben had spotted the canvas duffel, its contents protruding out of the partially zipped top. Positioned over it were a set of headphones, and the bag seemed to be wearing them.

Ben flicked the headset as he picked up the bag. In coming back to assemble the most important things she may have forgotten the first time around, Sage had chosen a Walkman. He had no doubt that the rattle from inside the bag indicated an assortment of cassette tapes mingled with clean underwear and lightweight blouses.

"I've missed my music." She shrugged as if reading his mind. "I thought as long as I was here . . ."

"You don't owe me an explanation," he teased with

the wave of his hand. "Far be it from me to separate a girl and her music just because her life is in danger."

"If you're a good boy," she taunted sweetly, "I might share."

He felt the wicked smile she flashed all the way to his toes. And the green of her eyes was as inviting as a fragrant meadow on a cool summer morning.

"I can only imagine," he muttered, heading out the front door. Then, as an afterthought, he turned to call back to her. "If you really want to treat me nice, you can sneak me a couple of those brownies."

"You got it," she said warmly, and he met her gaze.

Ben couldn't help take note of the bandaged area at the side of her forehead, and he winced inwardly at the reminder that anything or anyone had been able to harm her.

"Assuming Cook can be distracted," she added a lifetime later, then hopped down the hall like a child on her way to steal from the cookie jar.

Ben's heart skipped several beats as he watched her, then pounded that much harder to catch up. There was no doubt about it now, he knew. He loved this woman. And for the first time since she'd been taken from him, he did not feel the desire to apologize to Laura for moving on without her. Instead, he thanked her silently.

Chapter Fourteen

"**I** don't even know if it works," Ben told Sage when she began tapping at the cassette player in the dashboard of the old truck. "As far as I know, no one's even played the radio in here since 1984."

"Well," she sighed, opening the flap, and bit her lower lip lightly as she peered inside. "I guess there's only one way to find out."

She lifted her duffel bag to the seat beside her and began digging through it. "What would you like to hear?" she asked as she read the cassette cases. "I've got Talking Heads, Aerosmith, Eurythmics . . ."

"And?" he asked dryly.

Sage giggled. She might have known he was too stodgy and proper to settle there.

"How about Mariah Carey? Or Michael Bolton?"

"Mmm-mmm," he shook his head. "What else?"

"I know!" she cried, then produced a cassette from the

126

bottom of the bag and flicked it into the tape player hopefully.

The mechanism squealed as it began to turn, and Sage
poked open the flap with her finger to look inside.

"Didn't anyone ever teach you not to stick your finger
in an electrical appliance while in operation?" Ben said
as he quickly pushed her hand away from the dash.

"I think it's working," she said, ignoring his plea and
returning to her investigation.

She turned the volume knob slowly, and sure enough
there was sound! She looked hopefully to Ben for a long
moment until he nodded with recognition.

"Now there's something I wouldn't have expected,"
he told her. "You like Van Morrison?"

Sage nodded, then began to sing along with "Crazy
Love" at full voice. She wondered for a short moment
if he was thinking she should never quit her day job for
a singing gig, but she was having too much fun to let a
little ridicule stop her.

Halfway through the song, she leaned toward him and
said, "See. And I know all the words."

"I do see. Very impressive," he said, and she saw the
tiny turn at the corner of his mouth as he suppressed a
smile.

By the time the cassette had reached another selection,
both Ben and Sage were singing along with "Tupelo
Honey" at the tops of their lungs. They went through
several cassettes on the drive, and Sage put her head
close to Ben's on the harmonies, dramatically tossing her
arms about at the quicker rhythms. It didn't take long at
all for Ben to join in, and the two of them passed the
time in silly duets.

"A girl who carries a cassette tape of the Talking Heads and also knows all the words to Billie Holiday's *Come Rain or Come Shine*," he marveled, and she felt a rush of heat rise over her at the mere inkling that Ben was delighted at something—*anything!*—about her. "You're a fascinating human being, Miss McColl."

"Well, Mister Travis," she enunciated, "there are lots of things you don't know about me yet."

For instance, did you know that I've begun falling madly, head-over-heels in love with you?

"For instance?" he asked abruptly. "Do tell."

She paused, wondering if he'd read her mind.

Surely I didn't say that out loud!!

"This abundant supply of things I don't know," he prodded. "Dip into the well and share a bit."

Sage thought it over for a moment, then playfully produced another cassette from her bag.

"Okay, smarty-pants," she said, waving it at him. "I also have Louis Armstrong!"

Sage could hardly wait to get to the nursery once they'd finally made it back to the orphanage.

"I'll get my bag in a while," she called back to Ben as she marched double-time across the camp.

"You're back!" Larry called to her as she hurried by.

"Safe and sound," she returned.

"How's your father?"

Sage was torn. She wanted to stop and tell Larry everything about their trip, but there had been something pinching her at the center of her chest the entire time that she was gone and, although she couldn't pinpoint precisely what it was, she knew that holding Miguel again would alleviate the pressure.

"Well," she said, looking back at Ben who was quickly behind her.

Sage saw Maria standing quietly in the doorway to the classroom. They exchanged a smile and a wave, and she thought the girl looked beautiful in the pale yellow gauze dress she was wearing. Her hair was tied back with a bright blue scarf, and something in the girl's eyes was different, but Sage couldn't put her finger on it.

"Go ahead," Ben said, and with a smile she took off at a full run.

"How's my boy?" she teased as she entered, and Miguel jerked so hard toward her voice that he almost toppled over. "How's my boy?"

Gail grinned from ear to ear from her spot on the floor with several of the toddlers, including Miguel, amidst a set of wooden blocks. He began to giggle excitedly, using his fists to pound at the air, then forced himself into a speedy crawl across the floor toward her.

"Come here, come here, come here," she sang, then lifted him into her arms and twirled him around several times.

"He sure has missed you," Gail told her. "He just hasn't been the same boy."

"Did you miss me?" she asked him sweetly, then kissed the fine dark fuzz on the top of his head. "Oh, and I missed you, my sweet boy. Can I have a welcome home kiss?"

Miguel puckered up his mouth and planted a suction cup of a kiss on her chin that was dripping with saliva.

"Oh," she cried. "That's the best kiss I've had in my whole long life. Here's one for you!"

It wasn't until Gail said, "Where's Beth?" that Sage realized Ben had joined them, and he was watching her with delight—and something else—dancing in his eyes.

What was that she saw there?

"Sage's father is still in critical condition," he explained as Larry entered and joined the group. "Beth stayed behind to watch over him."

"Of course," Gail nodded, and Sage wondered if Gail and Larry had known about Beth and Mac, too.

Did everyone know but me? she wondered, and it gnawed at her that no one would have thought to tell her. *I have the most at stake, after all.*

"That little boy surely did miss you," Larry told her, nodding toward Miguel.

"So I've been told," she replied. "I missed him just as much."

"You'd better be careful," Gail warned with a grin. "You're not going to want to leave when the time comes."

Sage looked over her head at the battered, patchwork ceiling, then around the room at her shabby surroundings. There had been a time when she might have protested such an absurd notion, but now she wasn't so sure. Something about the place had sparked an inner fire, and it had the odd and almost-laughable quality of feeling as if she'd just come home.

"I'm afraid you're right," she admitted softly, then raised Miguel toward them. "Who could say goodbye to this little face, huh?" She brought the baby down and nuzzled his chubby little cheek. "My sweet boy. My sweet little boy."

She dropped to the large rug in the center of the floor and planted Miguel into her cross-legged lap where he happily remained. The other babies concentrated fully on pull-apart plastic shapes and knocking down piles of wooden blocks, but Miguel cared about nothing else except that Sage was home. As he formed an iron grip on two of her fingers, Sage's heart swelled up inside of her, and tears took a misty form in her dark green eyes.

"I love you," she whispered into his little ear, and she failed to notice the conspiratorial looks exchanged by the other adults in the room.

"Where do we stand since yesterday?" she heard Ben ask, then turned to find him walking out the door, his arm around Larry's shoulder.

"Here's what we can count on," Larry said seriously, then snickered. "Not one thing."

They shared a laugh as they exited, and Sage giggled at Larry's snorting harmony.

"Any good news?" she asked Gail when they'd gone.

"No, I'm afraid not," she replied, lifting one of the babies to the changing table. "It seems the Mexican government is bound and determined to get us out of here."

"But why?" Sage exclaimed. "It doesn't make any sense."

"Opposition doesn't have to make sense most times," Gail lamented. "It just has to be strong to win, and their case is very strong."

"Haven't they seen the children?" Sage asked her. "If they could just see them . . ."

"There are orphanages like this one all over the country," Gail explained. "All over the world, really. We'd heard rumblings for a long while. About five years ago, when Laura was alive . . ."

Gail stopped herself, and Sage looked up at her.

"I'm sorry," she said in earnest.

"Why?" Sage asked. "No need. I know Ben was married to the woman who brought this place together. I also know that he loved her very deeply."

"We all did," Gail added.

Sage looked down into her lap to find Miguel cradled there, his little head snuggled up to her chest, sound asleep. She watched his breath rise and fall for a moment before asking, "What was she like? . . . Laura, I mean."

"She was kind, and giving," Gail began, then moved over to the rocking chair nearest Sage. "She had this fine blond hair, like spun silk, and a tiny turned-up nose. Eyes so blue . . ."

The fog in her eyes told Sage that Gail had loved Laura very much.

"How long has it been?"

"A couple of years," Gail replied. "It seems like forever. I miss her so much."

Sage could only imagine, and her thoughts landed on Connie before she realized where they were headed.

"My best friend, Connie," she said, then stopped, silent.

"Did you lose her, too?"

"Yes," Sage said honestly. "But not to cancer. I lost her to something else. To opportunity. Or ignorance."

Gail didn't reply, just looked on lovingly, waiting for Sage to continue.

"But it's as if she's dead to me now," she finally continued. "And the pain of it is . . . well, it's terrible."

"It's always painful to lose someone you love, no matter what the circumstances," Gail said thoughtfully. "There is a grieving process, just like there is in death, and then you go on with your life."

Sage tried to smile, but her face curled into tears.

"I'm sorry if that sounds over-simplified," Gail comforted.

"No," Sage sighed in response. "It's not."

She didn't want to say the words. Even as they formed inside her head, she battled them.

I've grieved so many losses. I can't bear the one that might come next . . . I can't bear the loss of my father, too.

Chapter Fifteen

"**B**en, there's someone here you have to speak with!" Beth excitedly declared into the phone.

Beth was not one to over-dramatize, so Ben's heart picked up the pace a bit at the tone of her voice. He imagined for a moment that it would be Mac, that he would have awakened to find Beth at his side.

"Mr. Travis," a deep voice said into the phone, and Ben was almost certain it didn't belong to Mac. His heart dropped a bit as the man said, "This is Senator Rafe Blaine."

"Senator Blaine," he repeated. "What can I do for you, sir?"

He had seen this Blaine on the news a time or two. Politicians on the whole usually left him cold, but he recalled that Blaine's causes and concerns were usually very much in line with his own.

"Well, I came to the hospital to see about Mac," he explained. "He and I go way back."

"I understand there isn't much change."

"No. In fact, there's not. But while I've been here, Miss Wayans has been telling me about this orphanage problem you all are having down there."

"Well, it's a challenge, that's for sure," Ben replied, and the embers of his hope sparked a bit in the base of his stomach.

"Mac called me about your problem," the Senator continued, and Ben was startled at the information. "Not long before his accident."

Accident.

Ben repeated the word in his mind and wondered if that's what his friends had been told. Did they know it was Eric Randolph who had shot him?

"Now I can't promise you anything, you understand," Blaine downplayed. "But I am known for getting things done here in my home state. You just hang in there, boy, and let me see if there isn't something I can do to help out."

"Well, thank you, sir," he replied, his brows arched in pleasant surprise. "Anything you could do would be great."

The chances were that there was nothing that could be done from that side of the border, but the unusual fact that someone actually cared about his burden caused several pounds of weight to lift from his chest.

"Miss Wayans has pledged me her support," he continued. "She will work closely with me as I look into this . . ."

The politician in Blaine was plainly evident, making all the promises in the world without ever making a single one tangibly.

"... and let's hope we can do something for those precious little children down there."

So that was it! Blaine had zeroed in on the children. The visual pay-off for his good deed.

Whatever works, he thought, then thanked the Senator one more time.

Ben's morning runs had been non-existent while he was in San Diego, and he could certainly feel it now as he jogged breathlessly along the shore.

In the distance, he noticed the shadow of a form through what was left of the morning fog, and he instinctively knew that it was Sage before she came into full view.

She was carrying her tennis shoes, in much the same way she had carried those strappy stiletto sandals that first time he'd ever laid eyes on her, dangling from her fingers as she moved quietly through the dark house. Her hair was pulled back now into a loose ponytail, and her head was covered with the headset she'd retrieved from home.

"Morning," he called out to her, but he was no match for Talking Heads, or Aerosmith, or whomever had the distinct honor of crooning into her ear.

He watched her for a moment while he caught his breath. She seemed to be walking on water as she danced along the sand's border, kicking up splashes, pirouetting gracefully to the backbeat of music only she could hear.

She's so beautiful, he thought, then headed toward her at a slow run.

"Good morning," she greeted him, and she was his risen sun in that instant.

"Morning," he returned, and he watched her remove her headset. "Don't let me interrupt your dance time."

"Oh," she blushed. "You saw that."

"It was quite compelling," he said honestly, then wondered if she knew how true his statement had been.

"I was hoping the fog would shield me from anyone nearby," she admitted, then they shared a chuckle.

"So what are you listening to? Led Zeppelin? ZZ Top?" he teased, and she crunched up her nose and stuck her tongue out daintily.

"Neither, smarty-pants. I borrowed this tape from Gail. Listen."

Placing the headphones over the top of his head, she hit the button and let it play.

"Mozart," he commented, stowing away that happily stunned feeling that brought a flash of weakness to his knees. "You were dancing to Mozart?"

"It's great music, isn't it?" she said enthusiastically. "It's just so . . . life-affirming!"

"I heard from Beth this morning," she told him, and her ivy eyes lit up with joy. "Daddy's vital signs have improved. I think he's going to wake up, Ben. I really do."

Ben's heart soared.

And this is faith, Sage, he told her in his heart.

"I'm so glad for you," he said in earnest. "Any word on Randolph?"

"Not yet," she said, shaking her head. "But Daddy first. One thing at a time."

Yes indeed. One thing . . . one day . . . at a time.

Ben and Sage hiked back to camp together at a very slow pace. Ben told her all about Senator Blaine and his promise to make every attempt to assist them in their efforts, and Sage filled him in on Miguel's antics earlier that morning. The conversation was easy between them, from shared humor to mutual emotion. Sage thought that it seemed as if she'd known him her whole life.

"Do you think there's any way I would be allowed to adopt Miguel?" she asked, completely out of the blue.

"What? You want to adopt him?"

The surprise on Ben's face came very close to insulting. She felt instantly defensive.

"I'd be a good mother to him, Ben. I know I would."

"I'm . . . I'm sure you would, Sage."

"Is there any reason that I couldn't do that then?" she asked, her chin raised defiantly, her hands trembling.

"Let's see what our future holds," he replied finally, and she had to remind herself that he meant the future of the orphanage. Not the future of the two of them.

Sage avoided Ben for the rest of the day. She wasn't angry with him exactly, it was more like irritated. The look on his face when she'd mentioned wanting to adopt Miguel was one of near-disdain. As if the last thing in the world he could imagine of her was motherhood.

I'd make a fine mother, she thought. *But Ben Travis would rather that baby have no mother at all than have me for a mother?*

Suddenly, the bloom was off the rose. Just as recently as that morning, she had been enamored with everything about Ben, had even spent some time on the beach listing his good qualities, one by one. And then his reaction made her rethink every thought she'd had.

She looked out at the horizon, a smattering of pinks and purples and blues, and wished she had a camera. When the sun set in Mexico, it seemed bent on doing it with the kind of panache that called her to this place so often. Although she knew that California was famous for its own sunsets, a little trace of regret rumbled around inside of her at the thought of leaving the Mexican versions behind.

But leave it behind she would. Just as soon as Mac was out of the woods, and Eric was behind bars.

Sage closed her eyes and tilted back her head. The ocean breeze brushed over her like a silk scarf, and she inhaled a good, stiff shot of the salty air. It was so beautiful here.

"Hi."

The little voice came out of nowhere, and Sage shot up erect.

"Coco," she grinned. "You nearly scared me half to death."

The little girl backed away slightly.

"No, no," Sage told her, stretching her arms out toward the shy little girl. "Come sit with me."

Coco happily climbed up on the boulder and settled into her welcoming embrace. The two of them sat there for the longest time in silence, watching the orange ball of fire dip down toward the edge of the ocean.

"What are you daydreaming about?" Sage finally asked her. "Something lovely?"

"Sí," the girl nodded. "My green house."

"Your green house," she repeated. "Was that the color of your house before you came here?"

"I no remember casa before," she explained seriously. "But in my dreams, there is a green house to live in."

The contraction in Sage's heart was instant.

"This is a happy little scene," Ben said as he approached from behind, and Sage made a conscious effort not to let him see her entire body flinch at the mere sound of his voice. If Coco noticed, she didn't show it, and Sage was silently grateful.

He said a few words to Coco in Spanish that Sage thought had something to do with the sunset, and then his dancing eyes landed on her warmly. She was so lost in those eyes in that one moment that she almost didn't notice the book at the end of his extended hand.

"What's . . . ?" she began, then recognized it right away. "My book! Where did you find this?"

"That day with Randolph," Ben reminded her. "You dropped it on the ground while you were scuffling, I just . . . picked it up."

"Oh, Ben," she sighed.

How can I go from wanting to strangle him to wanting to kiss him in such a short span of time?

"I'd almost forgotten about it, but it was in the glove compartment of the truck."

"Ben, thank you," she said sincerely, then showed Coco the tattered leather cover. "I'd just bought it that afternoon when Connie and I were. . . ."

The thought of her friend was cut in half with sadness.

"Well," he picked up from there. "I thought you might enjoy having it while there's still light to read out here."

"What does it say?" Coco asked her in near-perfect English, and the girl's brown eyes shone with innocence as she peered up at Sage.

"Well, let's see," she breathed as she cracked it open to a random page. "These are love letters. Do you know what love letters are?"

Coco looked to Ben, and he translated. She gave a nod of understanding to Sage as she began to read aloud from the book. She knew Coco wasn't following, but the child seemed entranced by the sound of her voice, or perhaps just the moment of special attention shared with no other child.

After a few of the letters, Ben spoke softly to Coco in Spanish, and she nodded, turning to give Sage a brief but enthusiastic hug before running off toward the camp.

"Well, don't stop now," he said to Sage when they were alone. "Keep reading."

A little twitter at the center of her chest threw Sage a bit off balance, and she nervously tucked a wild lock of curls behind her ear.

"I'm serious," he grinned. "Read another."

Sage unceremoniously turned the page and landed on a letter which had been written by Fanny Kemble, an English actress from the 1820s, to her American husband, Pierce Butler.

"H-having loved you well enough to give you my life when it was best worth giving," she began, then looked up shyly at Ben before continuing. "Having made you the center of all my hopes of earthly happiness . . ."

Quick glances up at Ben between phrases stoked the

fire inside her heart, a blaze which was spreading, its flames fanning out to the recesses of her entire being.

" . . . I cannot behold you without emotion," she went on. "My heart still answers to your voice; the blood in my veins to your footsteps."

Sage closed the book and lifted her eyes toward Ben. She found it ironic that she had fallen randomly upon this letter in particular because that was much like what she'd been feeling toward him. As if she was on auto-pilot, and her reactions to him were unavoidable. He was the one. That was the plain truth, and there was nothing she or anyone else could do about it.

"I have one for you," he said, taking the book from her hands and setting it aside on the rock. He took both her hands into his and looked into her eyes deeply. She felt the warmth of his gaze, of his touch, throughout her entire body.

"Set me as a seal upon your heart," he said softly, his eyes never wavering from hers, his words touching a place in her heart she'd never known was there. "As a seal upon your arm; for love is as strong as death, jealousy as cruel as the grave. Its flames are flames of fire, a most vehement flame."

I'll say, she thought, and she wasn't able to move her gaze away from the hold he had on it.

"Many waters cannot quench love," he continued. "Nor can the floods drown it. If a man would give for love all the wealth of his house, it would be utterly despised."

He had fallen silent, at least to the physical ear, for several seconds before Sage finally spoke up.

"Th-that was beautiful," she managed, then tore herself away from the blue of his eyes, blue like the ocean, drowning her even now. "What is it from?"

"The Song of Solomon," he told her, then climbed up toward her and perched beside her on the boulder overlooking the last of the sun at the deepest edge of the horizon.

"That's in the Bible?" she commented, clearing her throat. She gave a nervous chuckle and shook her head.

"God's Word is filled with love," he said out into the ocean, never turning to look at her. "All different kinds of love. The love between a man and a woman is just one of them."

Sage's stomach lurched, and butterflies took off in a cacophony of fluttering wings inside her. It was several minutes before he spoke again, and the resonant sound of his beautiful voice rustled her heart as the light wind rustled through her hair.

"It's going to be dark soon. We should probably get back."

She watched Ben climb down from the rock, then reach upward toward her, offering a hand to help her down. She took it and landed on her feet before him. Their eyes met for only an instant, but it was a concentrated moment, a hole in time in which both of them knew what would happen next.

Ben took Sage into his arms and gently pulled her into a kiss. His lips on hers set the butterflies to dancing again, and his hand at the back of her neck, softly supporting, delicately massaging, sent electrical currents into every corner of her body. When it seemed as if the kiss would end, Sage grieved its loss before their mouths had ever parted. Seeming to sense her emotion, Ben trailed away with a dozen light kisses to the corner of her mouth, her chin, her jawline.

"I've been wanting to do that for a long time," he whispered, nuzzling his face into her hair.

"How long?"

"What?"

She'd startled him. But she wanted to know.

"How long have you been wanting to kiss me?"

Ben took her chin into both hands and stared into her eyes for a long moment.

"Since I was born," he said, and then kissed her again.

Chapter Sixteen

"Well, that's an improvement then," Sage cried hopefully into her cell phone. "Isn't it?"

"It is," Beth placated her, but the *umphh* just wasn't in the woman's voice to back it up.

"His blood pressure is normal, his heart rate is good," Sage repeated. "There is brain activity. That's all excellent news, Beth . . . What is it?"

She heard Beth sigh on the other end of the line, and her heart began to race.

"Is there something you're not telling me?"

"Oh, no, honey," Beth apologized. "It's just hard to see him lying there, so quiet and still. He's always been so vital, so alive."

"And he will be again," Sage stated, wordlessly demanding that Beth believe it.

Beth chuckled. "You're absolutely right."

"Beth."

"Yes?"

"Beth," she repeated, then paused. "I love you very much."

"Oh, honey, I love you, too."

"I just don't think I've ever told you how important you are to me," she said softly. "And with Daddy . . . well . . . I've just realized that you've got to tell a person while you can. You just never know when they won't be able to hear you anymore."

"Your father hears you," Beth promised. "And so do I. We listen with our hearts."

"Take care of him, Beth. And of yourself."

"I will," she agreed. "Love to Ben and everyone there."

Sage glanced at the small wind-up clock on the table near her cot and realized she was running late. She'd promised to relieve Gail in the classroom so that she could take Beth's cleaning duties in the mess hall.

Hurrying across the yard, Sage looked back to see an old junker of a car pull to a dusty stop at the top of the ridge. She smiled when Maria climbed out and jogged down the hill toward her.

"Hello," she called, and Sage noticed once again that something was quite different about Maria. She couldn't put her finger on it, but there was definitely something.

"Hi," she replied, then waited for Maria to reach her. "I didn't know you were coming today."

"I had afternoon free," she explained. "Señora Beth is gone, maybe you need help with the children."

"Do we ever!" Sage exclaimed thankfully. "Your timing is perfect."

Maria followed Sage into the classroom. Sage worked

with the older children on their varying levels of math assignments while Maria read to the third, fourth, and fifth graders from a Spanish history book.

When Maria's head rose and her expression turned excitedly hopeful, Sage scanned the room to find the source of her sudden joy. Her insides twisted sourly when she saw that Ben had stepped into the class, and, more importantly, was the catalyst for the young woman's brightening.

Immediately upon seeing her, Ben broke into a full, broad smile, shared only with Maria. A twinge of jealousy pounded in her temples, and Sage noted that a smile that big should have been reserved just for her. After that kiss, she was entitled to it. It was hers, not Maria's.

She watched as Ben opened his arms to Maria, and she ran into them at such force that he actually lifted her from the ground. They conversed in Spanish at the doorway for several minutes and, when Ben looked up to meet Sage's gaze, she jerked instantly away.

Her face and chest were flushed with heat, and the burning in her eyes spurred on a sudden throbbing headache.

"Can I tell Sage?" she heard him ask, and her palms went icy cold as the two of them approached.

"Tell Sage what?" she asked nonchalantly. But nonchalance was the last thing she was really feeling.

"I am to be married," Maria announced, then let out a laugh of joy and relief.

Sage looked at Maria blankly, then questioningly to Ben.

"Oh?"

"I allowed to marry because of you, Señorita," Maria told her frankly.

"Me?" Her blood began to rumble inside her. "I hardly think . . ."

"Juanita, my aunt, meet you and know Señor Ben not meant for me. So she agree I can marry Jose!"

Sage digested it for a moment. "Jose?" she repeated, relief running down her body like honey from the sky.

"Jose is the boy Maria is in love with," Ben explained. "Her aunt was holding out hope for her to marry an American, but she has now given her permission for Maria and Jose to marry."

There was the slightest trace of amusement in his blue eyes as he awaited her reaction, and Sage would sooner have walked across a trail of broken glass than let on how she was feeling just then.

"Congratulations!" she cried, then hugged Maria. "I'm so happy for you. When's the big event?"

Maria looked at her questioningly, and Ben translated in Spanish.

"Next month," she told them. "Church of my girlhood gone now," she added sadly. "We marry on town square."

Sage's heart began to soar, pounding wildly in her chest. She wasn't sure if it was Maria's joy which was contagious, or her own relief that there wasn't anything going on between the beautiful young girl and Ben.

"What did you think?" Ben whispered when Maria slipped away to the aid of one of the children. "That I was the intended groom?"

"Don't be ridiculous," she said, dismissive. "What an ego you have."

"Mmm-hmm," he jabbed. "I saw the look on your face, Sage."

She blew out a single puff of breath, tossed her hair back, and looked him square in the eye.

"You're too old for her anyway," she stated. "It would never have worked."

"No, you're right," he agreed. "What about you? Am I too old for you, too? Or is it you who's too old for me?"

"You know perfectly well that we're right around the same age," she scolded him. "What would make you say such a thing?"

"I like the way your fire-red hair stands on end when you get really mad at me," he grinned. "Is that a crime?"

"So you intend on goading me into anger every time you need a cheap thrill?" she snapped, then turned away to look aimlessly toward the children at their school-work.

"Nothing cheap about you, McColl," he whispered, and Sage turned to eye him curiously.

"I want to kiss you right now," he whispered even more softly, and the gleam in his eye did things to Sage she didn't even know were possible.

"Well, give yourself a minute," she said, turning away to camouflage the grin winding its way over her entire face. "You'll get over it."

The weather became so warm that afternoon that Sage shut down the classroom an hour early and organized the entire camp for an hour or so at the beach. Even the babies joined them, under the watchful eye of the adults and the older children. Coco was especially good with

Miguel, and Ben could see a joy in the young girl's eyes that hadn't been there since she'd come to them three years back.

"This good idea," Coco cackled as she hurried by in pursuit of Miguel, who was bumbling along the shore. "Miguel, wait!"

Ben's gaze was drawn to Miguel as the child's giggles rolled over one another with all the joy of the carefree boy that he was. He had no idea of the mysteries of the future, of the challenges of keeping the only home he'd known up and running. All he knew was love, and of this he had an abundance.

Sage joined the older kids out in the water, a volleyball game ensuing in no time at all. Once again, he marveled that she wasn't the same person he'd met in San Diego; she had changed so drastically. He would have liked to think it was him who'd had a hand in it somehow, but Ben knew that it was a greater power at work that was responsible for the transformation.

He remembered the kiss they had shared, and the helpless declaration she had made to him when she'd been rescued.

I love you, she'd said sleepily, and yet so convincingly.

He'd been carrying those words around with him ever since, guarding them as greedily as The Ark of the Covenant, for in those three simple words existed all hope, all joy, and all faith.

Could someone like Sage ever really love someone like me? he asked himself seriously. *This is a hard journey I've chosen. Could a girl like Sage ever accept it as her certain future?*

Although Sage had changed radically, Ben had to question whether the intensity allowed for a future of impoverished conditions, others' needs always coming before their own. He'd never had a single regret since committing to this life of service. Not even a question . . . until he met Sage.

She deserved it all. The house, the babies, the two cars in the garage, and Ben didn't know if he could ever provide such a life. His parents hadn't had a lot when they were raising Ben and his two brothers, but he never knew deprivation. He never yearned for something that he was denied, never woke up in the middle of the night with a hollow, howling stomach without the luxury of finding something with which to tame it.

This new sort of family he'd inherited from Laura was all of that, and more. And as small as the strides he had made were over the years, as minuscule as the progress in this work had turned out to be overall, Ben's heart glowed with satisfaction. He knew he had been doing what he was called to do. But meeting Sage brought with it the threat of change.

What would I do if I weren't doing this? he asked himself as Sage's laughter caught his attention and he watched her chase the children through the water, splashing and teasing and playing with complete and utter abandon.

He'd managed to eke out a degree from Bible school just after he and Laura had married, but his plans to get his doctorate were thwarted by the call of these precious little ones. They needed him more than any American church possibly could, Laura had told him, and he'd known that she was right.

He entertained a new notion for a moment . . . *Time to move on. Back to the States. Settle down and raise a family of my own perhaps?*

His gaze returned to Sage as she lifted Miguel into her arms and waltzed him out into deeper water, lowering his body all the way to the neck into the cool ocean. His squeals of delight seemed to spur her on, and Ben couldn't take his eyes away from them as they playfully splashed about.

I want to adopt Miguel.

He'd been surprised when he heard her speak the words. Not out of any doubt that she would make as fine a mother as there ever was, but because of the dramatic change in Sage's heart. She'd spent her first weeks at the orphanage doing everything she could to avoid the so-called "dirty work" of service in the nursery. She only held the babies when it was absolutely called upon, and even then it was at half an arm's length, like a smelly tennis shoe.

And now, as Coco, Mateo and several other children trotted through the water toward her, she seemed to be in her element as she welcomed them. It was as if this was where she belonged.

Ben's focus was drawn by a shrill sound he recognized as Sage's cellular phone. He quickly dug into the bag that rested on the blanket but, by the time he produced it from the bottom, the ringing had ceased.

"Sage!" he called out, and she waved at him happily. "Sage!" And he raised the phone toward her.

"Is it about Daddy?" she asked as she ran up to him from the water's edge.

"I don't know," he explained. "It was ringing, but they hung up."

"Oh."

"You might want to just call Beth to check. Maybe she has news."

Sage brightened at the idea, and plopped down on the blanket beside him before beginning to dial.

Her long sun-toasted legs seemed to stretch for miles, and the bright aquamarine swimsuit made it difficult not to inspect her more fully. Instead, Ben forced himself to look out toward the boys vying for Larry's attention as he tossed a football at random.

"Beth, it's Sage," she said, combing through her damp hair with soft, slender fingers. "Did you call me?"

She listened for a moment, and Ben saw her demeanor fall.

"Oh. I was out at the beach with the kids, and Ben said the phone rang but he didn't catch it in time. I'd thought it might be you."

She shook her head at Ben, and he was disappointed for her. He imagined that every ring of that phone brought the sudden expectation that Mac had awoken and was resting comfortably. And with every word that this was not the case, the disappointment dropped her just a little farther down her ladder of hope.

At that moment, the cell phone rang again, and Sage's eyes locked into Ben's as she depressed the button.

"Beth?"

Silence greeted her. But not the silence which accompanies a dead line; it was one of pure evil, and she recognized the presence immediately.

"Hello, muffin," Eric said, and the phone nearly slipped from Sage's hand. "Have you missed me?"

"You shot my father," she said coldly, and Ben moved stiffly beside her.

"Randolph?" he mouthed, and she nodded.

"It was an unfortunate turn of events, my dear. I never meant for any of this to happen. But, as you know, some mishaps just can't be stopped from snowballing."

"Eric," she spat. "Why are you calling me?"

"My intent was to get you to tell me where you are, my dear," he stated, the height of calm. "But I'd expected to have to cajole you. I didn't imagine you would tell me first thing."

"What are you talking about?"

"Well, when you picked up the phone, you called for Beth. Could that mean you've been hiding away at her little orphan camp? The one she wanted Mac's money to finance?"

Sage's blood ran cold. "He knows where I am," she mouthed to Ben, her hand shielding the phone.

When she reached up and held on to his forearm, he covered her hand with his own and squeezed reassuringly.

"A pity," Eric crooned. "All of those innocent little children in the line of fire."

"If you dare harm anyone else, Eric . . ."

"Well, perhaps we could reach an agreement," he suggested smoothly. "No one gets hurt, and you and I leave peacefully together."

"So you can finish what you started?" she asked incredulously. "I don't think so."

"So that I can explain my side," he corrected. "Make

sure you understand my way of thinking. We can do this easily, Sage. Or we can do it rough. It's your choice."

The look on her face told Ben she had taken all she could. In one movement, he took the phone from her hand and pressed the button to disconnect. Sage just stood there for almost a minute, her hand still frozen in the air where it had held the cellular phone.

"Ben, he knows where I am!" she cried at last. "I've put all of you in danger. I've put the *children* in danger!"

"Shhhhh," he said softly, pulling her into the embrace she eagerly sought.

"He'll mow down anyone who gets in his way," she deduced. "My father is a perfect example of how far Eric is willing to go."

"It's going to be okay," Ben promised authoritatively, smoothing her hair and massaging the muscles at the back of her tight neck.

Then, after a few moments had ticked by, he raised the phone and began to dial.

"Who are you calling?" she asked.

"Detective Ray Martin, please. It's Ben Travis."

Chapter Seventeen

Beth's cot hadn't seemed so empty to Sage in all the time since she'd come back from San Diego without her. The moon was high and bright silver that night, and it carved beams out of the darkness in the room through the slats of the shuttered window.

Beyond Beth's neatly made cot was a third one, and Sage watched Gail's chest rise and fall with every breath. Normally, she shared the tiny room behind the nursery with her husband; but tonight she wanted to be close to Sage, and Sage needed her to be.

In the dark of night, the distant hum of insects harmonizing with the faint rattle of waves at the shore, Sage was frightened. Anything could happen now that Eric knew where she'd been hiding.

If only I hadn't said Beth's name, she chastised herself. *I should have been more cautious.*

So very many people had been affected by the wrong

choice Sage had made in Eric, each of them in the path of this avalanche that thundered uncontrollably over anything and everything in its way. She'd lost Connie because of it, or at least the idea of Connie. She suspected they had never been as close as she'd believed. She had almost lost her father, too. And now Ben and Beth and the children were in danger as well, and she silently rued the afternoon she'd met the distinguished and mysterious Eric Randolph.

She realized now that it was his checkbook she'd been drawn to—his powerful presence rather than anything tangibly appealing. He made her feel important. People looked up to him, she had thought at the time. Now she realized it was more fear than respect.

Sage rolled over on the cot and looked up at the sky through the one shutter slat that was slightly askew.

She wished she hadn't promised Ben that she would stay put after dark, because she had an almost irresistible urge to creep over to the nursery and look in on her little Miguel.

She imagined him sleeping there in his crib, his dark lashes fluttering as he dreamed of a world of castles and giant wooden blocks, rocking horses and trumpeting horns. Sage smiled at the fantasy, then found herself wishing she could have such sweet, childlike dreams as well.

When this is all over, she thought, and then stopped herself for a moment. Did she dare take a chance on reaching out for such an impossible dream?

Her dreams were riddled with audacity these days. She went so far as to fantasize a future with Ben that involved children and marriage and love and laughter.

She'd indulged the fantasy a time or two before, but now, this night, it seemed so far out of reach she could barely touch it.

At any moment, Eric could burst in and drag her screaming into the night. If she screamed, someone would come, she realized. It could be Ben or Larry, or even one of the children! And there was sure to be bloodshed.

No. I will not scream, she promised herself then. *Even if it means going with him. I will not scream.*

A sudden chill of fear moved over her like a wet woolen blanket, and, raising herself to sit cross-legged on the cot, she peered into the shadows of the darkened room. The breeze tossed loose brush against the far wall outside, and her heart pounded relentlessly until the sound stopped.

So many things I might have done differently, she spoke from her heart. *So many people I've hurt.*

Stephen came to mind immediately, and she silently confessed her poor treatment of that dear man. He would have been a good husband to some other girl, someone who could appreciate his giving nature, who could support him and stand quietly at his side. Someone who would remain at the altar long enough to say, "I do."

How humiliating it must have been for him, in front of all his friends and family, to turn to the woman he loved only to see nothing more than a streak of white retreating down the aisle and out the back door.

"Why did you let it go on so long then?" he'd asked her later. "Why didn't you just tell me you were having doubts?"

Sage dropped her head into her hands and began to

weep as Connie's face crossed over her mind's eye. She had been a part of every important day of her life, whether glorious or tragic, and Sage had honestly loved her deeply. Now she wondered if she hadn't been quite the fool for doing so.

The night seemed to go on forever. An endless parade of memories, twilight shadows and muted sounds, each of them with the potential of turning into Eric at a moment's notice.

"Sage?"

She sat upright and her breath froze in her lungs.

"Sage, are you awake?"

Letting the breath out at last, she answered, "Ben? Yes, I'm awake."

She could barely make out his shadowy form as he entered, but she would have known it anywhere. Quietly, he eased down to the cot beside her and rubbed the length of her arm poking out from the oversized T-shirt. The spicy scent of him calmed her like the most soothing treatment of aromatherapy.

"I couldn't sleep," he confessed, and she agreed.

"Me either."

"I had to see you."

Wide-eyed, she waited for him to tell her why.

"Sage, I'm in love with you," he forced out. "I am. I love you."

All the times she had imagined this moment, and now it was here . . . and all she could do was stare at him.

"How do you feel about that?" he asked her curiously. "Is it something that . . . you . . . would like?"

"Yes," she said immediately. "I love you too, Ben."

Ben took her face between his two hands and guided her into a kiss, soft and sweet.

"I know I can't offer you the things that you deserve," he began, and her heart soared at the knowledge that it no longer mattered. "I don't know where life is headed tomorrow, or next week. The business with the orphanage, then your father, and Randolph. Everything is in so much flux, and yet . . ."

"And yet?" she gently prodded.

"And yet I want to know—*I need* to know—that, as we go into this uncertain territory, Sage, we enter in together."

What was he looking for, she wondered. *A commitment to couplehood? A promise of something. But what?*

Anything was her heart's reply.

"I know I have nothing certain to lay before you," he continued. "Except this one thing. I will love you until the last breath I take. I couldn't be more certain."

"Oh, Ben . . ."

"Marry me, Sage?"

Her equilibrium tilted for just a moment, and a fog of tears rose in her eyes. "Yes, I will."

Ben put his arms around Sage and held her to him.

"Miguel and Coco," she whispered hopefully. "Can we adopt them, Ben?"

He tilted her chin upward and looked hard into her eyes.

"I know I can be a good mother to them. I know I can."

"I know that, too," he said softly. "We'll make it happen."

And she suddenly believed him with all her heart.

"I have something for you," he said, digging into the front pocket of his bleached denim shirt. "I hope you'll take this in the right way because I give it to you only in love. I want you to know that."

"What is it?" she asked curiously.

"Here," he said, then placed a delicate gold chain into the palm of her hand. Dangling at the end of the chain were two tiny charms. A gleaming cross, and a golden key.

"It's beautiful."

"It was Laura's," he said softly. "I gave it to her on the day we were married. And now I want you to have it, Sage. You are the keeper of my heart."

"Ben," she breathed, and she thought that it was the most wonderful gift she had ever received.

Ben held her for a long time, and then in a whisper, so that only the two of them could hear, he spoke of love and hope and faith. And then, together, they prayed. For Eric's capture, for Mac's recovery, for the fate of the children. And they prayed for grace to handle whatever paths they were to journey down together.

Several hours later, Sage's eyes fluttered open to find herself upright, leaning into Ben's chest, his arms set loosely around her, breathing slowly, deeply.

We fell asleep, she realized, and then the shrill alarm sounded again. *What is that?*

Sage bolted toward the sound, snatching up her cell phone on the box table next to her cot.

"Yes?" she said tentatively as Ben, awake now, moved in closer. "Detective," she said into the phone, then her eyes locked with Ben's.

Perhaps the moment was all wrong to be noticing the tiny flecks of gold in his blue eyes, or the deepened hue as he awoke from sleep, but Sage noticed it just the same and held it fast to her heart.

"What did you say?"

"We've got Randolph," Ray repeated. "We caught him trying to cross the border."

"He was coming for me then," she realized, and a shudder of fear rattled her to the bone.

"He was indeed," the detective confirmed. "But Ben's quick thinking in reporting the call Randolph made to you gave us time to anticipate that move. We caught him at the border at 2:15 this morning."

"I'm so relieved," she said, then smiled broadly at Ben. "They have him in custody."

Ben's expression exploded with joy. He pulled her in close to him and began kissing her hair, her forehead, her nose.

"Let me talk to him," he said between kisses and, giggling, Sage handed him the phone.

"My hero," Ben teased as he turned the phone in his hand so that Sage could hear, too. "Good work, Detective."

"We make a pretty good team," Ray admitted. "I was just telling Sage, we might never have caught him in time if you hadn't thought so quickly to report Randolph's phone call."

"But you did catch him," Ben said. "I owe you more than I can ever possibly repay."

"All in a day's work for a superhero," Ray joked. "Will she be coming home?"

Ben looked at Sage briefly, then darted his gaze away. "I suppose she will, yes."

"Good. She'll want to make herself available to the prosecutors. Have her give me a call when she gets in."

"Will do," Ben said softly. "And Ray. What about the Vesper Diamond?"

"It's still out there somewhere," he replied. "See you later."

"Later."

"What's all the noise?" Gail asked from her cot, as she began to stretch and yawn.

"They caught Eric," Sage said excitedly. "They found him trying to cross the border."

"That's wonderful!" she cried. "I'm going to go tell Larry."

They watched her slide into the tennis shoes at the end of the bed and adjust the sweatsuit she'd worn to sleep. Blowing a kiss to them from the doorway, Gail was gone.

"I should call Beth," Sage said, and she was already dialing the phone before the words were out. "Do you think she'll be at the hospital or at home?"

Ben didn't have a chance to answer before Sage made the connection.

"Beth! They caught Eric," she cried. "I can come home!"

Like a left hook that landed directly above his ribs. That's how those words felt to Ben as Sage uttered them so enthusiastically.

I can come home.

The bitter taste of resentment rose in the back of his

throat. He'd proposed to her that night while they awaited the news, and she'd said yes. But now, in the light of day with Eric Randolph safely in custody, all of that seemed . . . forgotten.

I can come home.

As if it had been her fondest desire, come to life.

Of course there was her father, Ben reminded himself. She would want to be with him now. But she hadn't uttered a word about their engagement to Beth, all the while she sat there on that phone, mindlessly twirling the cross around her neck as she uttered those horrible, haunting words.

I can come home.

And Ben knew that she would do just that. Once she realized how little impact his proposal had actually made on her, she would probably say something polite, like, "I need to be with my father now. I'll miss you. I'll call every day."

And then she would be gone.

Women like Sage didn't settle for men like Ben. He imagined he would be chalked up in later years as some sort of mistake, a man in the right place at her most wrong time.

Like . . . what was his name? Stephen.

The man she'd left standing at the altar. Beth had told him all about it, long before a trace of his feelings for Sage had boiled up to the surface. He imagined the man had been dull, much like he himself was dull, in comparison to the rest of Sage's glamorous life.

Yes, dull. That's how his small life must have seemed to Sage. He was a religious man, after all. And weren't they known world-over as the dullest people of all?

I wouldn't trade one day, he thought angrily. *If she doesn't want to be a part of it, then so be it.*

Yes, Sage was sure to make polite excuses, but Ben knew for certain when she left for San Diego, she would probably be leaving him as well.

Ben made the announcement at breakfast. All of the children lined up to get a last hug and a cheery smile from Sage as they said their good-byes. She would be leaving that very day.

He sure didn't waste any time, she thought as she watched Ben standing back, looking on as if observing from on high. *He's completely removed from me now that he doesn't feel he has to protect me from anything.*

"I come with you," Coco offered sweetly, and she held tight to Sage's hand.

"Oh, honey," she replied, kneeling down before her and taking the girl into her arms. "You need to be here. Your friends are here, and your lessons. You need to practice your English so that we can have a girl-talk when I get back."

Coco's lashes brushed her cheek as she stared down at the floor.

"I come with you," she pleaded, and Sage thought her heart would break into splinters right then and there.

"I won't be gone long," she promised. "I just have to go and be with my father now. He's sick."

"Papa sick?"

"Yes. But I'll be back."

Coco muttered something in Spanish, and then looked up at Sage with accusation in her eyes.

Sage shook her head. "I'm sorry, I don't know what that means."

"She wants you to promise her," Ben said from behind her, and she looked at him curiously. "Promise her that you'll come back."

"I promise," Sage vowed, and traced an X across her heart.

Coco produced a folded sheet of paper and extended it toward Sage. She took it, unfolded the paper, and looked from it to the child and back again.

"What's this?" she asked, managing a smile.

Coco didn't respond. She just looked hard at the dirt beneath her, sneaking a quick glance back up at Sage as she investigated the picture Coco had drawn for her.

A large green house with white shutters and a flower garden filled the page. Stick figures lined the front yard: a man, a woman, a girl and a baby.

"Oh," Sage gasped, and tears began to fall spontaneously.

So this was what Coco had been dreaming. Funny how they'd been sharing that dream without ever really knowing it.

"Is that you?" she asked, pointing to the larger of the two children depicted.

"Si," she nodded. "Y Miguel, y Señor Ben, y Sage."

Sage opened her arms to the child, who fell into her and wrapped her arms so tightly around her neck that Sage had to pick her up in order to stand upright.

"I love you," she soothed. "I love you."

Something in Ben's eyes as he watched them startled her. As if he were angry. Or hurt.

Perhaps all these good-byes are just hard for him.

Men are such babies when it comes to watching someone show real emotion.

Gail walked with her up to the nursery and Sage paused at the door before going inside.

"Miguel is going to be so sad to see you go," Gail said, taking Sage's hand. "You take care of your dad, and come back to us very soon."

"I will," she nodded, and the two women hugged enthusiastically. "Thank you, Gail. Thank you so much. For everything."

"Be good," the woman smiled. "I'll let you have some time alone, and I'll come and relieve you in half an hour."

"Great."

It didn't help her resolve any when Miguel immediately raised his arms to her as she stepped through the doorway. She was crying before she ever reached the crib, and she picked him up and held him to her tightly.

"I'm going to miss you, little guy," she sniffed. "I can't stand the thought of even one day without your smile. Your kisses."

Miguel heard the word and knew its meaning. He puckered up spontaneously and planted a loud smack at the side of her nose.

"Right," she chuckled. "Kiss."

The word had a far different meaning for Sage than it did for Miguel.

Kiss.

She knew she'd never hear the word again without conjuring up instant, smoky visions of Ben.

A breeze of sweet peace rested on her just then, and

Sage lowered into the rocking chair, clutching Miguel to her chest.

Ben had changed the moment Eric was caught. And he started arranging my trip home before we'd ever even discussed it, she thought. *He's had second thoughts. And this is his way of letting me down easy, by sending me home.*

Sage fingered the gold cross and key hanging around her neck and wondered for a moment if she should give it back before he sent her away.

No, she decided. *I'll have Beth bring it back later.*

She couldn't face such a task just now. Although she yearned to be at her father's side again, her heart ached with the knowledge that, when she left Mexico behind, Ben would most likely leave all thoughts of her behind as well.

What would become of her dreams then? Visions of a life with Ben, of motherhood and wedded bliss, fell like rain before her. Holding Miguel close, Sage began to cry.

Chapter Eighteen

She'd left him her cell phone, with all the pertinent numbers, but Ben hadn't called her once in the three days since she'd left him standing at the bottom of the embankment. He'd said things to her like, "Be happy," and "I'll always love you," but she could plainly see that he was saying his final good-byes.

No mention was ever made of his marriage proposal, and it stung wickedly at Sage's core. Fidgeting with the chain that hung loosely around her neck, she sniffled back the deep sadness threatening to reappear.

"Oh, Daddy," she said to him, but she knew he couldn't hear. "I love him so much."

She stroked his warm hand, then used the blanket to dry off the tears that had fallen upon it.

"I don't know how it happened," she continued. "One day I thought he was this staunch man of God—someone

I could never have seen myself with—and the next, I was planning a life with him in my head."

Sage blew her nose, and then tossed the tissue into the trash before continuing.

"He's a good man, Daddy. Loving and kind. He would have treated me with respect and . . ."

She stopped herself. The pain rose up inside her like a wave, crashing down with a clatter.

"But he doesn't want me any more," she told his sleeping face. "I guess he was sort of a savior type, huh? And while I was in danger, he was my white knight or something. But once they'd caught Eric, once I didn't need protecting anymore, his feelings changed in an instant. He didn't have the heart to tell me, but I could see it in his eyes."

A flash of crystal blue eyes and a fringe of golden lashes caressed her mind.

"He has beautiful eyes, Daddy. Sky-blue, with little flecks, just like gold dust."

Tears spilled out of her eyes once more, and Sage lowered her head, dropping it onto her folded arms on the side of the bed. Her entire body wracked with sobs and, despite her efforts to the contrary, they were loud and inconsolable.

Something inside her told her it was good to cry, good to let go of the emotions that had been holding her captive, although she'd been doing a good bit of it already since returning to the States alone. Sage allowed herself to cry even harder then, releasing all of the fear, the pain, the resentment and the humiliation. But try as she might, she simply could not release the one last thing that held her prisoner.

She could not release Ben.

"I love him so much," she sobbed. "What am I going to do, Daddy? I wish so much that you were here to tell me what to do."

As Sage was blowing her nose one last time, something caught her eye. She looked at Mac, sleeping and still. Just at the moment she had decided it was her imagination, she noticed it again.

"Sage."

She could hardly believe it when Mac's eyes began to flutter open, and his hand moved stiffly into hers.

"Daddy?" she cried, standing up to lean in over him. "You're awake. You're here!"

"Sage," he spoke again, and then tried to smile at her.

"Oh my gosh," she cried with glee, and then pushed the call button to the nurse's station. "Daddy!"

"Wh-what are you . . ." he struggled.

"I'm right here, Daddy."

". . . crying for?"

She was so relieved that she burst into laughter. The irony of it overwhelmed her.

"Sorry, Daddy. Did I wake you?"

A windstorm of doctors and nurses and aides worked around her, taking Mac's vitals, checking his bandages, writing up reports, calling for bloodwork.

"Beth," she said into the telephone on the nightstand. "Get over here right away. Our miracle has happened. Daddy's awake."

When a small window opened within the wall of people around Mac's bed, she saw him looking at her through it, and he smiled.

"I love you, Daddy," she mouthed, and he returned the sentiment with a precious nod.

Joy flowed over her until she was almost taken under by the emotion. Her father was awake!

She had to call Ben.

"That's wonderful news," he had said, but there wasn't an ounce of *wonderful* showing in his voice.

It had taken more than twenty-four hours to reach him, and the least he could have done was feign excitement for the most miraculous news she'd had in her whole life.

"Is something wrong?" she asked with an edge to the question.

"No," he assured her. "I'm very happy for you. I know this is your fondest wish."

"Can you come up, Ben?"

She'd been afraid to ask him, so when it came out at last, it came as almost a whisper.

"Do you *want* me to come up?" he asked, and she sighed.

"Of course I do."

"I have some things to clear up here first," he replied. "Let's talk about it in a couple of days."

She didn't want to wait. Even if he came just out of nothing beside common courtesy, she would take whatever she could get.

"Any progress with the Mexican government?" she asked.

"Nothing but opposition," he told her frankly. "And we're coming down to the wire."

"Oh, Ben, something will happen. A miracle. I just know it."

"I pray that you're right," he said tiredly.

"I'll talk to you in a day or two then," she surrendered, then waited for his reply.

Tell me you love me. Say it, Ben. Please. I can live forever on those words if you'll just say them.

"Good-bye then."

"Good-bye."

Sage wandered back into her father's hospital room in time to catch the tail-end of a kiss shared with Beth. It did her heart good to see someone's love going right, especially since hers seemed to always go so dreadfully wrong.

"Come on in, honey," Beth beamed, and Sage noticed that they were holding hands.

"You look perky and flushed today," Sage said. Then she grinned as she added, "You too, Daddy."

"Come here and give your old man a hug," he invited, and Sage thanked God as she did just that.

"Mac McColl, you old dog!"

They all looked up to find Rafe Blaine standing in the doorway, his white hair as perfectly coiffed as always, his dark chocolate eyes twinkling with glee.

"Rafael, you old coot, get in here!" Mac said, chortling, and the Senator leaned over Sage to shake his friend's hand and slap him gently on the back.

"Beth was just filling me in," Mac told him.

"Yes, we've had some mighty fine discussions while you've been AWOL," Blaine clucked. "This is a fine woman, McColl."

"Don't I know it."

Sage marveled at the pure happiness resonating in her father. She couldn't remember the last time she'd sensed anything like it from him.

"And you, little lady," he directed at Sage. "Glad to hear your troubles are behind you."

"Yes," she nodded, noting that her troubles with Ben had only just begun. "Me, too."

"So is this a friendly hospital visit," Mac asked hopefully, "or do you have some news to share?"

"A bit of both," he beamed.

"Tell us," Beth breathed excitedly.

"Two weeks," he stated, and they all looked at him curiously.

"What's in two weeks?" Sage asked.

"Two weeks' time," he explained, "and we can bring those little ones of yours across the United States border."

"What?" Sage was rapidly on her feet. "What are you talking about?"

"Beth," he seemed to chastise. "You haven't told Sage our good news?"

"I was waiting for something definite from you, Senator," she told him with a gleaming smile.

"Well, you've got it now. You tell them the good news, and I'm off for a round of golf with the governor."

"Tough life, politics," Mac joked, and the two men shook hands one more time.

"Good to see you, dog."

"Good to be seen, coot."

"Beth, what is going on?" Sage demanded the moment Blaine had left the room.

"Well, the Senator has used his considerable influence

with the Mexican government, as well as our own, to grant our request to relocate the orphanage to American ground," she said, pausing to share an excited smile with Mac. "We've found this amazing old Victorian house on the north side that was a shelter for unwed mothers until just a few months ago when they moved to a larger facility in La Jolla. The Senator is seeing to it that we receive U.S. funding for the orphanage, and it's big enough to house every child we have in residence."

"And they're going to just let us take them out of the country?" Sage asked skeptically. "They're Mexican children."

"I don't know how he did it, honey. I'm just thanking the Lord that he did."

"When Rafe Blaine says he'll do something," Mac interjected, "that man will do it."

"Does Ben know?"

She couldn't help but ask, her thoughts turning back to him the way they always did.

"No," she explained. "He knows the Senator has promised his support, but he has no idea that he's been able to pull it off."

"You two will have to get down there pretty quick," Mac told them. "There will be a lot to do before bringing them up here."

"Forget it."

"No way."

They voiced their objections simultaneously.

"Daddy, I'm not leaving you until you're out of this place and safely tucked away at home."

"Oh, yes, you are," he told her seriously. "Ben needs you."

Sage looked to Beth, and then to her father. She hadn't told Beth about Ben's proposal, nor about his subsequent rejection.

"What do you mean?"

Mac turned to Beth with a chuckle. "The girl comes to my room, sobbing, crying, telling me, 'Daddy, I love him,' 'Daddy, he doesn't love me,' wailing at the top of her lungs so I had to come out of a coma to tell her to be quiet . . ."

Sage let the tears fall, and simultaneously giggled at her father's rendition of her bedside confessions.

"You heard that?" she asked him, then turned mock-serious. "Oh, you were just dreaming. I wouldn't have done that."

"You would and you did!" he accused joyfully, then looked at her quite seriously. "You do the right thing, my girl. You go down there and be with the man you love."

Ben had tried to tell himself that he could handle seeing her again; that it was no big deal really. He'd showered and shaved and put on his best khaki Dockers with the green knit sport shirt she'd liked so much, and now he checked his watch every other minute between glances upward to the top of the hill.

Where are they?

He reminded himself that he had to thank her for the senator's intervention. It might never have happened if not for Sage and her father. He looked around at his surroundings and his heart softened suddenly. It would have done Laura's heart good to see that these twenty-eight children were going to the home country she had held so dear. These children, at least, would break free of the poverty and primitive surroundings. It had been her dream for as long as Ben could remember. And later it had become his own as well.

Gail was setting out large bowls of tortilla chips and smaller dishes of salsa on tabletops decorated with colored paper and balloons when the first of the three vans came into view atop the embankment.

"Larry! Ben!" she called out. "They're here."

Carrying Miguel up the hill toward them, Gail waved frantically. The moment the passengers began to deboard, Beth, Sage, Gail, and Miguel had closed their ranks in an ecstatic group hug.

"There's my little man!" Sage cried, taking the baby into her waiting arms.

Ben swallowed back emotion as he watched at a distance, then waved back to Beth as she headed down the hill. Suddenly, she turned back and then shrugged at Ben animatedly when Mac pushed away the wheelchair being offered.

"I don't need that contraption!" he heard Mac insist. "I'm a grown man, I can walk down a hill."

"A grown man who was in a coma until two weeks ago," Beth objected. "Will you set your duff into this chair so we can get down there and greet the kids?"

Mac obliged reluctantly, and Beth hurried down to embrace Ben while Larry lagged behind to push the chair.

"I've missed you," Beth told Ben. "And so has Sage."

Missed me so much she only called once, and that was to tell me the news about the senator's efforts.

"I've missed you, too."

And it was no lie. Beth had become somewhat of a maternal figure to Ben, and her absence was felt as keenly as . . . as any other.

"Hello, Ben."

He blinked when he saw her. A vision of color and vibrancy and beauty. His voice clung to the back of his throat, and his palms instantly turned icy hot.

"Sage," he nodded. "Welcome back."

It was at that moment that Coco spotted Sage, and her gasp drew everyone's immediate attention.

"Señorita Sage!" she screamed, then clumsily stumbled into a hug.

"I told you I'd be back," Sage giggled. "Did you miss me?"

"Sí!" the child assured her with enthusiasm. "Oh, sí, sí!"

"And did they tell you about the new house?" she continued as she walked away, holding Coco's hand. "It's called Green Way! It's the green house you've always wanted!"

The party was a time of true celebration, for everyone except Sage. Ben was a million miles away from her, even though he sat just beside her at the head table.

Lunch consisted of frankfurters which were grilled outside, corn on the cob and honey-baked beans. The children thought it was the best thing that had ever happened to them, but Sage was at the other end of that spectrum. She felt as if she were living out some horrible nightmare, so close to Ben and yet so distant that she could hardly reach him.

The plan was to load up the vans after they had eaten,

and to reach the U.S. border just before sundown. Beth had shown her the paperwork, and Sage didn't expect there to be any trouble with the border patrol.

Some time after lunch, Sage decided to take a final walk out to the beach. The ocean seemed to call out to her, beckoning her near for one last word. Sage planted a kiss on her father's cheek before setting out, then ambled across the sand toward the shore.

"Don't be too long," he called after her.

"I won't."

She saw Ben there long before he saw her. His back was angled away from her, and he was leaning down slightly, backlit by the warm afternoon sun. The scene signaled something profound inside her heart. She feared that in the next moments, she would see the end of a dream as it unraveled before her into the sand. She would have to leave Ben there at the edge of her familiar ocean, along with all thoughts of a life together, with Miguel and Coco as their perfect little ready-made family, with the other children's future families hanging in the balance.

It was amazing to her how solid those dreams had become in such a short time, how suddenly maternal she had become, how natural it had seemed to take on the role of mother to Miguel and Coco, wife to Ben. And how shattered those visions were now.

Unclasping the necklace as she approached, Sage fought back the wave of emotion she'd thought she'd wrestled under control on the long ride from San Diego.

"Ben?"

He looked up suddenly, and their eyes locked tight for a long moment.

"One last look?" she finally asked.

"Yes." He peeled his gaze from hers and stared out at the water.

"This is an important place for you, isn't it?" she said softly as she perched next to him atop the familiar boulder.

"For me, for Laura," he confirmed, and her heart lurched.

"Speaking of Laura," she started, then extended her hand toward him, the gold necklace resting in her palm, "I thought you might like to have this back."

Ben looked at her as though she had slapped him hard.

"I know its meaning," she told him. "I didn't think it would be fair to keep it."

"Fine," he snapped, taking the necklace from her hand.

She watched him for a long while as he toyed with the necklace, focused on its shine.

"Well," she said after several minutes. "I guess I'll head back."

She waited again, but nothing. So she lifted herself and dusted the sand from her skirt. She hadn't taken five steps away from him when Ben's voice rose behind her.

"What happened, Sage?"

She turned to see that he was on his feet, his fists clenched slightly, confrontational in his stance.

"They caught Eric, your dad made it through," he said accusingly, "and you didn't need me anymore?"

"No, I . . ."

"Was it that easy to just toss me aside and hightail it out of Mexico as fast as your little legs would carry you?"

"Ben, you've misunder—"

"I haven't misunderstood anything!"

"You have," she insisted. "And you're the one who proposed to me one night and then sent me on my way the next!"

"You were going anyway."

"Yes, I was," she admitted. "I had to be with my father. But I wasn't leaving you. I said I'd come back."

"And you did do that," he replied bitterly.

"Ben . . ."

"Forget it," he said, and she watched his body freeze into a solid block of anger. "Just forget it all."

She wondered if she should leave it alone and just walk away, but suddenly she couldn't. She wouldn't.

"I don't want to forget it, Ben. I want to love you. I want you to love me again. Tell me what went wrong. Talk to me so we can try and fix it. I just want you . . . to love me . . . again."

He looked at her curiously, and he looked more handsome to her in that moment than he ever had before. The sunlight danced through the highlights of his dark blond hair, and the tiny, familiar twitch at the corner of his mouth set her heart to racing.

"Again?" he repeated softly. "Did you think I ever stopped?"

"Yes," she nodded sweetly, and tears broke free from her eyes.

"No," he said, moving slowly toward her. "I never could."

"Ben."

"I love you," he said directly into her eyes, and she curled her arms around his neck gleefully.

"But can you live out a life with a man like me,

Sage?" he asked, pulling her away to look at her seriously. "It's not an easy life. It's not a life of privilege."

"The question isn't whether I can live my life with you, Ben," she told him tearfully. "It's whether I can live my life without you. And no, I can't."

His face told her all she needed to know as he swept her up into his arms and kissed her thoroughly. She was dazed and her lips were swollen when he was through, but what he did then brought her to full and complete attention immediately.

Dangling the gold necklace from his fingers, Ben sweetly said, "Will you marry me?"

"Sí, señor," she nodded happily as he put it around her neck. "Sí."